RITA LONGKNIFE:
ENEMY IN SIGHT

BOOK TWO OF THE ITEECHE WAR

MIKE SHEPHERD

KL & MM BOOKS

Honor Harrington with her strength and intelligence. Mike Shepherd provides an exciting military science fiction thriller." -Genre Go Round Reviews

"'I'm a woman of very few words, but lots of action': so said Mae West, but it might just as well have been Lieutenant Kris Longknife, princess of the one hundred worlds of Wardhaven. Kris can kick, shoot, and punch her way out of any dangerous situation, and she can do it while wearing stilettos and a tight cocktail dress. She's all business, with a Hell's Angel handshake and a 'get out of my face' attitude. But her hair always looks good . . . Kris Longknife is funny and she entertains us." - SciFi Weekly

"[A] fast-paced, exciting military SF series . . . Mike Shepherd has a great ear for dialogue and talent for injecting dry humor into things at just the right moment . . . The characters are engaging, and the plot is full of twists and peppered liberally with sharply described action. I always look forward to installments in the Kris Longknife series because I know I'm guaranteed a good time with plenty of adventure." -SF Site

In the New York Times bestselling Kris Longknife novels, "Fans of the Honor Harrington escapades will welcome the adventures of another strong female in outer space starring in a thrill-a-page military space opera." - Alternative Worlds

"Military SF fans are bound to get a kick out of the series as a whole." - SF Site

COPYRIGHT INFORMATION

investing in a copy so I can continue to earn a living at this
wonderful art.

I would like to thank my wonderful cover artist, Scott
Grimando, who did all my Ace covers and will continue
doing my own book covers. I also am grateful for the editing
skill of Lisa Müller, David Vernon Houston, Edee Lemonier,
and as ever, Ellen Moscoe.

Rev 1.0

eBook ISBN-13: 978-164211-0159
Print ISBN-13: 978-194211-0081

ALSO BY MIKE SHEPHERD

Published by KL & MM Books

Kris Longknife: Admiral

Kris Longknife: Emissary

Kris Longknife's Successor

Kris Longknife's Replacement

Kris Longknife's Relief

Rita Longknife: Enemy Unknown

Rita Longknife: Enemy in Sight

Short Stories from KL & MM Books

Kris Longknife's Maid Goes On Strike and Other Short Stories:
Vignettes from Kris Longknife's World

Kris Longknife's Maid Goes On Strike

Kris Longknife's Bad Day

Ruth Longknife's First Christmas

Kris Longknife: Among the Kicking Birds

Ace Books by Mike Shepherd

Kris Longknife: Mutineer

Kris Longknife: Deserter

Kris Longknife: Defiant

Kris Longknife: Resolute

Kris Longknife: Audacious

Kris Longknife: Intrepid

Kris Longknife: Undaunted

Kris Longknife: Redoubtable

Kris Longknife: Daring

Kris Longknife: Furious

Kris Longknife: Defender

Kris Longknife: Tenacious

Kris Longknife: Unrelenting

Kris Longknife: Bold

Vicky Peterwald: Target

Vicky Peterwald: Survivor

Vicky Peterwald: Rebel

Mike Shepherd writing as Mike Moscoe in the Jump Point Universe

First Casualty

The Price of Peace

They Also Serve

Rita Longknife: To Do or Die

Short Specials

Kris Longknife: Training Daze

Kris Longknife : Welcome Home, Go Away

Kris Longknife's Bloodhound

Kris Longknife's Assassin

The Lost Millennium Trilogy Published by KL & MM Books

Lost Dawns: Prequel

First Dawn

Second Fire

Lost Days

Captain Rita Nuu-Longknife sat back in the rocker that had been added this cruise to her in-space cabin. She struggled to compose herself, to relax herself. She did not want her baby to take in her tension with his mother's milk.

One of the nannies she'd brought aboard the heavy cruiser *Exeter* brought little Alex in. He was fussy. Rita hoped he was hungry, she had two painfully full breasts she should have given him to suck an hour ago.

Now she offered her infant son a breast and he latched onto it hungrily. He calmed as he nursed, but he showed no sign of falling asleep. His deep blue eyes gazed up at her.

"What are you doing on a heavy cruiser?" Rita asked her child. Little Al made no reply. Of course, the question really wasn't aimed at him.

The question was for Rita.

She, herself, as assistant Minister for Exploration, had found the money to bring this war relic back into commission, fit it out, and bring a crew aboard. That done, she'd demanded the right to command and gotten it from a Navy that only let women skipper attack transports.

Since the *Exeter* wasn't bound for war, at least not yet, she'd been allowed to command it. She'd also gotten away with bringing an infant aboard so she could nurse him.

She got the ship, and she got to go exploring.

The fruit of her exploration was in the wardroom freezer, and several other freezers scattered around the ship. The *Exeter's* exploration had not led to rich new planets ready to receive hearty colonists who were eager to make a life for themselves out on the rim of space.

No, Rita had found what she was looking for and praying not to find. She'd discovered the wreckage of a human ship, blown to bits so tiny it took all her science team's forensic skills to find out its type and place of construction. Of its crew, there was not a scrap of flesh or bone left to see.

Several systems over, they'd found the evidence that an impossible story told by wild-eyed pirates was true.

Again, the forensic team went through the wreckage of a ship. This one was less shot up, but that did them little good when it came to finding which human planet had built it.

The metal was all wrong. The food, the equipment, the wiring . . . even what was left of the reactors . . . all was wrong. This ship was not a product of a human shipyard.

But they already knew that.

They'd found the bodies, preserved in the freezing vacuum of space. Bodies like none anyone had ever seen. Skulls with four eyes and a beak where a nose should be. Torsos with four arms that ended in hands with four fingers. Hips with four legs that ended in feet like none that had ever walked the Earth. And don't even try to count all the elbows and knees!

Captain Rita Nuu-Longknife had discovered what she'd commissioned the *Exeter* to find. She'd found what she'd taken her tiny son to space in search of.

Humanity was not along. Not anymore. First contact had been made by a bunch of bloody minded pirates looking for loot.

Could the rest of humanity now find some way of reaching out peacefully to the first species we'd ever met in space? Alternately, were we condemned to meet our first alien contact with fire and blood?

2

Geneneral Ray Longknife, formerly of the 2nd Guard Brigade, Wardhaven Army, and officially the assassin of President Urm of Unity . . . it was in all the papers . . . scowled at the star map he'd been annotating. He started it as a work in progress shortly after Rita left to check on the pirate's story.

He did not like the story it told. Or maybe refused to tell.

He'd included all the ships that he knew had gone missing in the last three months. He'd started with the *Prosperous Goose*, way off somewhere between Santa Maria and the rest of human space. He'd added a ship here, another there, as reports of vanished ships made it to his desk.

So far, he didn't have that many red X's.

What he did have was a bright yellow dot representing a single, questionable, ship of unknown origin.

Of late, he'd had to add a new color. Orange markers now showed planets that had been raided by pirates, their crops stolen and, in some cases, men and women carried off.

Too damn much of the sphere of human space was being blotched in one color or another.

A few were on the far side from Wardhaven around the rim of the human sphere of colonization. Most however, were somewhere along his side of humanity's spread among the stars.

Ray studied the map for a long five minutes. When he was done, he didn't know anything more than he had before.

The only easy pattern was that most of the trouble was on his side of human space.

Beyond that, not so much.

Andy, retired captain from the Society of Humanity's Navy and Ray's number two man at the Wardhaven Ministry of Exploration, knocked and came in without waiting to be told to.

"I have a bit of something from your friend, the spy."

Ray let his eyebrows crawl up his forehead. The spy had no name, at least not one anyone remembered. He ran the Wardhaven Intelligence Bureau, and occasionally he knew stuff before the people who would be doing a task knew what they were going to do.

"What rumor has he deigned to drop on us today?" Ray said, dryly.

"He has a list of private survey ships that have gone missing," Andy noted. "Twelve of them."

"A full dozen!"

"Yep, by my count."

"Can you add them to the map or do we have to do it the hard way?"

"Let's see how good I am with this newfangled technology," the retired Navy captain said, and rested his reader near the net access point in front of Ray.

The two systems beeped happily at each other for a few

moments, then a series of red loops began to connect stars on Ray's map.

"Those were the jumps they were supposed to take out from and back to human space," Andy said.

Ray studied his map again. The red loops led to a certain section of space. True, it was a wide front, covering a good quarter of the sphere that humans had claimed by labor and goods for themselves. The red loops spread wide and covered a large area, but it was certainly showing a pattern.

Finally, the dozen vanished ships and the missing exploration ships began to make a picture that spoke to Ray.

"Notice something?" Andy asked.

"Which something?" Ray asked.

"You tell me," Andy said.

"About half, maybe a bit more of the ships that went missing are in human space," Ray said.

"Yep," Andy agreed.

"How much you want to bet me those were taken by our pirates?"

"No bet," Andy said with a friendly grin. The man had bet his life against Ray's proud Guard Brigade and won. He claimed he'd used up all his luck beating Ray, and was likely right.

"Smart man," Ray agreed. "Now, these other ships. The *Goose*, and the *Witch of the Westmorlands* out of Lorna Do, and all of the dozen the spy just got his hands on, they're way out there."

"And notice," Andy said, "that the *Jackpot No. 27* passes only a couple of systems away from where the *Bucket of Blood* claimed to pop an alien."

"Yeah, I noticed that," Ray said.

"Who do you think we ought to show this to?" Andy asked.

"Let me call my father-in-law," Ray said, and tapped his commlink. "I'll see if he can drop by here ASAP."

3

Ray was not at all surprised by who showed up for his meeting with Earnie Nuu, his father-in-law.

The spy arrived before Earnie did. He eyed the star map, smiled and asked where the Scotch was. Ray pointed him in the right direction. The spy expressed delight at the amount of ice on hand.

Ernie was next, but walking in his shadow was the platinum blond. Today she wore a dress that was bright red and short at the bottom, plunging at the top. The teenager in Ray found himself hoping for something to come up or fall down, but the more mature Ray was pretty sure what he saw was all he'd see tonight.

Behind her were Red Tie and Blue Tie. These two strange, non-communicative men and the no less expressive platinum blond were his conduits to the Powers That Be in the Society of Humanity. At least, that was what Ray suspected. The two guys headed for the liquor cabinet. Ray held out a chair, then seated the young woman. The first and only time they'd met, she'd been quick to assert that she was somebody's wife. Ever the officer and a gentleman, he asked her what she would like to drink, and then provided her with a white wine, no doubt of a poorer vintage than she was used to.

When everyone was served, Ray turned the briefing over to Andy. He quickly went through the identified locations or routes of lost ships: humanity, and the one potential alien.

"What are the orange lights?" the woman asked.

"The pirates have taken to raiding the newer, outer colonies for food and the occasional workers or pretty girl. At least all but one of those lights involve an agrarian planet. The single exception is Leadville, a mineral extraction site with its own smelters that produces a refined output of iron, silver, gold, titanium, and the like. I suspect the pirates' yard wanted the raw feedstock to repair some of their ships."

"And gold, no doubt," the woman said, then took a sip of her wine. "What is a pirate without a little gold?"

"Most pirates I've met preferred briefcases," Andy muttered softly.

The woman smiled, but made no comment.

"So," Ray said, bringing the meeting back to the map. "The losses in our own space can likely be laid at the pirates' door. It's the deep losses that remain a question mark to me. Also, I think you should note the closeness of the alleged location of our destroyed alien ship to one of the missing human scouts. *Jackpot No. 27*, as you may note."

"You think the alien we killed may have first killed one of our scouts?" the lady asked.

"There's no way to possibly draw any conclusion, other than to say that that part of space is getting a bit rambunctious."

"Rambunctious. A good word," she said, and again sipped her wine.

"What do you propose to do?" the spy asked.

"Just what I've done," Ray said. "I've correlated all the data that has surfaced at the moment. I've handed it back to you. All of you," he said, glancing around the group.

"Now, I suspect that you will pass it back up to your interested parties. I'm working with the Navy here on Wardhaven to get a half-dozen heavy cruisers away from the pier and out there, patrolling our immediate space, but I'd like you to point out to anyone you talk to that the ships that went lost on deep scouting missions may well have been lost very deep. The *Bucket of Blood* may have been about as deep as any of these when she ran into her reputed alien."

"What are you getting at?" the woman said, putting down her wine glass. It was still much more than half full.

"The depredation on our colonies are coming from humans. We have witnesses that tell us that humans landed at their towns, emptied their grain silos, slaughtered their cattle and pigs and stole their daughters. That's something we humans have been doing to each other for a very long time. We should do what we've always done to put an end to it."

Ray paused to do a check of his listeners. As he's expected, Ernie was all with him. The rest, from the spy to the beauty to the two ties were blank faces. He'd have better luck getting a reaction from a fire plug.

No, he'd get water from a fire plug. He'd get nothing from these four.

"As for the attrition to your deep scouts, that's another matter, and one I think we ought to examine carefully. Do we want to keep sending ships out to get picked off, or is it time for us to put together a fleet of contact? A decent sized fleet with some serious technology and ethnographic experts to see how well we can do with our first aliens."

Ray eyed the non-reaction he was getting, and chose to

give them nothing back in return. Then he had a stray thought.

"I'm assuming that none of you have got a ship back that reported shooting it out with some strange ship and winning?"

The three, red dress and both ties, actually had to glance at each other.

It was a while before the woman said, "We'll have to talk about that, won't we boys?"

"Yeah."

Ray was a soldier. Soldiers lived and died on whether the intelligence was good or bad. Their life depended on the man to their right and the woman to their left. He'd had about enough of this selfish shit.

"People, folks are dying out there. Can you at least agree to give me the data I need to keep more from dying? Have any of you got a ship back that shot it out with a round ball of fuzz and lived to tell of it?"

The three of them stood, shared not a word with Ray, and left.

"That didn't go all that well," General Ray Longknife said, stalked to the liquor cabinet where he poured himself a tall Scotch over very little ice.

"You got their attention, General," the spy said. "Before you popped your little question, I doubt either of those three factions had considered it. Now, it's out on the table. I suspect there will be some serious discussions tonight."

"But will there be any trust behind the words?" Andy asked.

"And will it matter?" he added. "Often, when a ship takes a hard hit, the reactor loses its containment and you don't want to be around when thermonuclear hot plasma gets loose in your ship."

"What you're saying is that just because one of their ships survived a fight with an alien ship, doesn't mean it knows any more than our pirates knew when their fight ended," Ernie said.

"Less," Andy said. "Our pirates got a picture of an alien body. If a ship blew from the reactor out, there may be nothing left bigger than an atom."

"So, again I ask," said the spy. "What do we do now?"

"We wait for my wife to get home with our son and tell us what she saw," Ray said. He took a sip of his drink, thought some more, then downed the rest in one gulp, "and hope she's willing to leave the rest of the recon contact to someone else."

Ray went to refill his drink. Maybe he'd see something in the map when he was roaring drunk that had evaded him when he was stone cold sober.

4

Captain Edmon Lehrer, the very titular head of this pirate kingdom thanks to murder and assassination, finished counting the raised hands of the captains at the table. Most had a bottle of rum in front of them. The three woman captains had red wine.

"I see twelve hands for us moving farther out to the new base," he said.

The grunts from around the table concurred.

"So, the count of captains is twelve that we stay here at LeMonte and twelve that we move our base to Port Elgin." Captain Lehrer glanced around the bare bones conference room on their bare bones space station and said. "Ladies and gentlemen, we are tied."

"So twelve of us will go," said Captain Maynard, the spokesmen for the Port Elgin faction. "Ed, you ain't been nearly as bad to work for as Whitebred. And smarter than him, but face it, it's best if we do split up."

Lehrer shook his head, but only a bit. "There's strength in numbers, Billy."

"There's also advantages in keeping a lower profile,"

Captain Maynard said, continuing the pre-vote debate. "You been shearing a lot of sheep in this neighborhood. Do that too often and somebody's bound to holler. If we move out a bit and over some, we'll be shearing a whole different herd. And besides, Ed, Port Elgin is pretty damn near heaven itself."

"Yeah," one of his supporters jumped in. "You can swim in the ocean. Eat the fish. Hell, half the stuff growing on the trees there you can eat."

"The half that don't kill you," came from one of Lehrer's supporters.

"Nobody died."

"They just wished they had as they tossed up their toenails."

"So, we don't eat that one again."

"Okay, okay," Captain Lehrer said, pounding the table with a wooden door knob someone had found on a captured ship. "The count is even. Half of you captains will go. The other half will stay. For the crew, we'll let them vote with their feet. If some of yours would rather stay, we'll find a berth for them. If any of ours want to join you, they're free to go."

"And we'll find a job for them with us," Maynard agreed.

Lehrer took a deep breath, and prepared for what might bring them to blows. "Billy, the station will stay."

"I never said it wouldn't, Ed. Hell, we had enough trouble setting it up; no way would I try to stuff it back in a box and take it out of orbit."

"Good," Lehrer said, and found he was letting out a deep sigh. Then he went on with the practical matters. "You know you're going to need to work on your ships sooner or later."

"And we'll pay well to have the yard here do the work.

It's damn sure we can't go anywhere else." That drew a laugh.

"And Ed. All of you," Captain Maynard said, sweeping the table with a sincere smile. "If it gets too hot here, you know where you'll always be welcome."

Maynard nodded. So far, the route through the nova and nebula had stayed a secret. "Billy, I'm more afraid of them chasing you down."

"We're going out far enough that they'll be hunting for us until long after we die of a happy old age," the other pirate captain assured him.

"Okay, Bill. When do you intend to pull out?"

"It will take us a day to get the other icicle ship ready to move again. Thanks, Ed, for letting us have half the laborers."

"Even if this place is as nice as you claim, I still suspect you'll like an occasional good old Earth dinner."

"Yes, we will."

They settled the rest of the outstanding matters without coming to blows. It hadn't come to that yet. Fights at the captains' table? Not quite.

Still, maybe it would be easier to manage things when they were down to only twelve.

Edmon Lehrer snorted softly at the thought. They were pirates. No pirate wanted someone to tell him what to do.

Captain Rita Nuu-Longknife was overjoyed to see Ray waiting for her on the pier as the *Exeter* was drawn into its berth. As was traditional, some of the best optics on a warship were focused on the dock as crew searched for their waiting loved ones.

Just because she was the skipper didn't mean she was immune to an ancient Navy tradition.

The fact that Ray was not alone was to be expected. Her mom and dad were there, no doubt waiting to get their first look at Alex in far too long. He'd taken his first step, or so the nannies told Rita.

He had yet to take a step with her in attendance.

The spy was there, as well as a most striking platinum blond who was way too close to Ray. What had she said about what was good enough for the goose being fine for the gander?

Well, Ray better give her his full attention. She'd sent ahead a very brief message that they had found the target. If anyone wanted to hear more, they better come to her.

And they did.

Her mother was ushered off to the nursery, but the rest were directed to the *Exeter's* wardroom. While they waited, Rita oversaw the change of her ship from underway watch to in port watches, as well as the engineers putting the reactors down for their nap.

Actually, the ship's three reactors never fully went off line. One or two might be cut out for maintenance, but one was always up, running at least a trickle of plasma around a superconducting magnetohydrodynamic race track to generate electricity for the ship's needs.

Only when all her duties as a ship's lord, master, and captain were complete did she breathe a sigh of relief, adjust her uniform and head for the wardroom.

Her breasts were feeling full, but she'd expressed extra milk so Alex wouldn't go hungry. No doubt, her mom would be in heaven to have a chance to feed her first, and so far, only grandchild.

Rita would make sure the meeting did not run too long. A nursing mother with an uncomfortable pair of breasts was even more motivation to short meetings than an old man with a bladder problem. No doubt about it.

Rita entered the wardroom to find that Matt had already made it over from the *Northampton*. Ving was over from the *Second Chance* as well. Both had brought a major portion of their science teams with them. Boffins, as Matt called them.

None noticed as Rita entered the room; all were congregated around not the coffee urn, but the large screen that took up a chunk of the wardroom's forward bulkhead.

Rita was getting herself some coffee when she recognized the screen as a star chart. And the section of stars represented by it.

She forgot the need for coffee and headed for the projected star map.

Her husband spotted her. His eyes lit up and his worried mouth twisted into a bright smile. She found she was giving him just as bright a smile right back. If she wasn't careful, they'd start acting like just two kids in love, not two senior officers that should set their subordinates a good example.

"Folks," Ray's command voice carried. "Let's take our seats. It's better we give you a full explanation of the map so that you can give us a full explanation of what you found out there."

People broke for chairs, still the three ship's companies managed to sort themselves out and seat themselves together. Rita found herself unexplainedly relieved when the stunning platinum blond in the tight electric blue dress settled into a chair beside the spy. Ray waited for Rita to take a chair, then booted Hesper out of her chair so he could sit beside her.

"Andy, you're getting good at this briefing. Do it again," General Ray Longknife ordered.

The retired Navy captain brought Rita up to date on what had been going on in human space while she'd been busy. Andy showed the proposed search sweeps of missing exploration ships but did not explain how they came to have the trip plans for a dozen privately funded exploration voyages.

"What's the name of that ship that went close to our alien hot datum?" Rita asked. "By the way, the wreckage wasn't there, but three star systems over."

"That's the *Jackpot No. 27*. Missing from Savannah."

"Was it a Daring class cruiser by any chance?" she asked.

"No, it was a General class cruiser," the retired Navy captain said without having to refer to notes. "That class they built before the Daring, although I'm told they were a lot alike."

"Well, they are, and we found a chunk of it."

The ships' crews were ready for that, but it ran like wildfire through the folks that had just come aboard, which she saw now included her dad.

"Well, captain," her husband said, "why don't you fill us in on what you found."

Rita stood, and went down the short list of what they knew about the alien ship and the wreck of the *Jackpot No. 27.* "Crazy as it may seem, the aliens appear to use salt water for their reaction mass."

"Salt water?" came from most of the Wardhaven contingent.

"There is definitely sodium in their reaction mass. Why?" Rita said, and shrugged. "Your guess has to be better than ours, but I won't take any bets."

Ray and Andy just shook their heads.

"Hey, they're alien, so expect something alien from them," Rita put in.

"Do you have any of their bodies?" Ray asked.

"There are about a hundred of them in our freezers," Rita said.

"Can we have priority access to a dozen of them?" the woman in the bright blue dress asked.

Damn, even her voice is beautiful, Rita thought. *Who are you?*

Ray didn't introduce her, but nodded. "You have first call on a dozen. After that, you have to wait in line."

"A dozen will satisfy the labs we have lined up on Earth and a half-dozen other planets," the woman said.

So who is your 'we', lady?

The lady didn't say and Ray didn't ask. *Ray, we have to talk when this is over.*

"Doctor Qin, would you care to report on what we do know about the aliens?" Rita said.

"They are big, and have very well-developed musculature. In a physical encounter, they would likely win unaided by weapons or technology. Their DNA bears no relationship to ours. We doubt there is any way for a human and one of these to exchange germ material."

"Huh?" the spy said.

"No way will there be babies between us and them," Rita translated.

"Oh," several of the civilians said. Rita noted the platinum blond did not react to the translation. Either she got it the first time or she was too cool to let surprise show.

You're good. I hate you being anywhere near my husband, but you're good.

"We found several other examples of animal life that shared the same DNA history with the aliens, although we expect they were no closer to these aliens than, say a pig or chicken is to us. They appeared to have been alive when they went into space, so we think the aliens like their food raw. It's possible that they were storing fish like food in their reaction tanks and that might explain the salt water."

"An interesting hypothesis," the spy said.

"It's little more than a guess," Doctor Qin said.

"We'll accept guesses for now. We can reject them or not when we get more data," said the spy.

Dr. Qin went on with a short list of what they knew and a long list of what they didn't before sitting down.

Rita stood up again.

"So, there you have it. We do indeed share the galaxy with another space faring race. How good they are is still a question on the table. What they're intentions are toward us is also an unanswered question. We've collided with them and blood has been spilt. Not a lot so far. However, if we don't do something about it, there may be a whole lot more. May I suggest that our first order of business is to put our own house in order while we see what more we can learn about these aliens?"

"Put our house in order?" the blond asked.

"Put the pirates out of business before they kill any more of these aliens," Rita snapped. "If ever we needed a single policy initiative, we need one toward the aliens. At least we're all one big, friendly Society of Humanity now. The sole exception to that seems to be the pirates who, it seems, are also searching the same space."

"We'd prefer to see some immediate effort made to meet these aliens," a civilian in a gray suit with a blue tie said.

"I think the captain has a good point," Ray countered, in more of a growl than the voice Rita usually expected from him. It was also nice to see him backing her up.

"Please, boys, the captain and her husband have a good point," was not the back-up Rita wanted. It came from the gorgeous blond. "It shouldn't take much of an effort to suppress the pirate problem. Certainly not if we make it a concerted effort."

"Are you going to back closing down the exploration missions?" snapped the fellow in a red tie. Rita studied the three civilians, two males and one female. Expensively dressed, they were young, too pretty to work for a living, and, apparently, not on the same team.

"No one from any association is trying to tell anyone else what to do," the young woman said easily. "Still, we all have to agree on a unified policy, or we all have to agree we are free to go our separate ways. However, it seems to me that we can all agree that getting enough of a Navy out to put down the pirates would be a good idea. As to our different exploration efforts, so long as everyone continues to report their voyage plans so that if your ship goes missing, we know where to look for the aliens, it's no skin off anyone else's nose."

She finished with a smile that emphasized her pretty little nose. Rita fought to like the woman she so wanted to hate.

"I'm not so sure I agree with you on that last matter," Rita said. "We've gone over all the machinery and electronics we salvaged from the alien wreck. For now, we can't make any sense of it, but that doesn't mean we won't succeed if we keep on trying. The same thing applies to the aliens. The more of our gear they find in our wrecked explorer ships, the more chances they have to find out something important about us. Like where we live."

That sent a noisier wave of discussion around the wardroom than Rita was used to having in one of her Navy meetings, but this one did have a batch of scientists as well as a few humans that were acting like a bunch of kids that had never learned to play well in the sandbox.

Which left Rita promising herself that she'd see that Alex did learn to play well with others even if she wasn't there to watch his first step.

Something was clearly wrong with this picture, but Rita was busy at the moment and needed to chase down her present set of problems.

"I don't know who you work for," Rita said, rising her voice to be heard above the low roar, "but our first meeting with aliens needs to be handled well. So far, it's being botched. Would you please tell whoever your associates are that we need to speak with one voice and act with one accord?"

The three too-pretty civilians looked at her like she was a mentally deficient child.

Her father stood. "The captain has a point. I'll see that it is carried to the highest levels of your three associations. For now, I'm asking you to hold up all scout initiatives for a month, two weeks at least."

Red Tie looked about to come out of his chair. The woman threw him a look, and Blue Tie rested a restraining hand on his elbow.

"Two weeks," he muttered.

"That will give me time to see that the captain's reasonable concerns are raised to the highest level," Ernie said.

"Now, about the pirates," her father continued.

"I've met with Admiral Zilko of the Wardhaven Navy," General Ray Longknife said. "He's fitting out six heavy cruisers to go pirate hunting. He'll need money to pay for the steaming days, though."

"I think we can get an allocation of funds from the Society's Navy appropriations," the platinum blond said. The first thing Rita had heard from her that she liked.

Maybe you're not all bad. Just don't look at Ray like that.

"That will go a long way towards us getting our house in order, as the captain so wisely put it," General Ray Longknife said. "First, we put down the pirates, then we send out a task force to see where these big fellows come from and say 'hi, we want to be friends'."

Ray would remember those words a lot in the coming years.

6

C aptain Maynard hammered for silence. He didn't have the wooden door knob Ed Lehrer had, so he hammered with the butt of his pistol.

We're pirates, what better way to make noise?

But before each meeting, he was careful to take the magazine out and clear the action.

Right now, he was about ready to reload the pistol and fire off a shot.

Ed could never have done that on the station. There were benefits to being on a planet.

And Port Elgin was a beauty of a planet. The meeting hall was just a few logs holding up a roof made from tree branches that almost looked like palm fronds. The place was open to the sea breeze and the sunlight reflected off the harbor where the ships' shuttles were drawn up.

Hell, even the farmers were having it easy. All you had to do was drop a seed in the ground and it sprouted in no time. Several were actually putting on weight even though they'd raised a bumper crop of the drugs.

The only question was would any of the shit get bailed

up and hauled off for sale back on Earth or one of the other big markets?

If the story he'd just heard was true, maybe it didn't matter.

Pirate Captain Maynard slapped the magazine into the butt of his automatic, chambered a round and fired a shot through the frond-covered ceiling.

"Shut up," he shouted into the duller roar.

Things actually got quiet. Captain William Maynard gave the hall his best glower. It stayed quiet. Each and every one of the captains crammed around the table or the small mob standing around ten or more deep were just as eager as any captain to hear if the latest rumor was true.

Come to think of it, having all this space is a bitch. Ed could have just us captains in his conference room. I must have half the crews and not a few of the farmers listening in.

"Okay, Captain Ben Hornigold, can you tell me how you just happened to sneak up on this planet full of gold? I mean, if there were really alien ships around it, how'd you get in close."

Captain Hornigold bristled where he stood.

"Don't get me wrong, Ben, I ain't calling you a liar or anything. I just want to know."

Bill's question was back up by a lot of "Yeahs," "Right," and even a "Nobody's that lucky."

Ben hitched his belt up, and let his hands come to rest near both of the pistols at his waist. "We was lucky," he said. "And smart. None of yous dumb guys could have pulled off what we did."

That got a lot of people talking to the person next to them, but the room seemed more interested in hearing what he had to say, so it quieted.

"Yeah, we spotted a strange ship. Not much more than a

ball. Nothing like you'd think a ship should look like. Anyway, we was just coming into a system as it was jumping out. So real quick, we jetted over and took a peek at where it went."

Ben paused to give the room a wide, toothy grin.

"And jumped right back out of that system. Hell, there was three of them round ships in orbit around one planet. Now, that might have been it, but we got this great kid for a navigator. Yee ain't much to look at, and he don't got a lot of schooling, but he likes to read and he knows star charts. He comes to me with this idea that we duck around, do five jumps and come back at this star system from a different direction."

Now the meeting hall was overflowing with murmurs of admiration. Beside Ben, this short thin, beanstalk of a kid with black hair was beaming.

Captain Ben seemed to enjoy being the center of attention. It was a bit before he went on. "By the time we got around to the back door, all the ships was gone, so we kind of tiptoed up to orbit the planet and took ourselves a good look at it."

"Didn't they spot your approach? Give you a call?" Captain Bequia asked.

"Nope. No radio calls. No radar. Tell me, if all the ships was out, what kind of lookout do you keep here at Port Elgin?"

That kind of put the kibosh on the talking for a moment while people looked around. Some of them even looked thoughtfully.

Bill made a note to himself to do something about that, though there was usually a ship or two in orbit.

Yeah, but how many of them have an active sensor suite going?

"Once we gets into orbit," Ben went on, "we looked the place over real good. There was this town, of sorts. It looked thrown together, just like Port Elgin do. There was some poor dumb sods scraping in the dirt, but there were just as many standing up to their knees in the river that ran by the place. From where it emptied into the sea all the way up about a hundred klicks. Lots of folks panning the gravel."

Ben patted the skinny kid on the shoulder. "Reads-a-lot here said that was how you find gold, and damned if we didn't when we sent a longboat down, real careful-like, to get the lay of the land. Yep, that river was running with gold."

"You sure it's gold?" put in Bequia.

"Not even Reads-a-lot could answer that, but we brought it back and one of the icicles was a chemist. We thawed him out and he says it's gold. Even did a test on our nuggets. You better believe it's gold," Captain Ben Hornigold said, proud as paint.

He paused for a moment to hitch up his gun belt again before continuing. "There's a mountain of silver too that they're digging out. That and I don't know what all. I tell you, they are sitting on a mother lode of shiny shit."

The room exploded in talk.

Bill ignored the talk. He locked eyes with Ben. Ben looked right back at him. Then the two of them nodded.

In one voice they shouted, "Shut up."

And for the first time Bill could remember, the pirates shut up.

"Okay, they are sitting on a pile of shiny shit," Bill said. "What do they do with it?"

"Just about all of them have a gold or silver chain around their necks," Ben Hornigold said. "And they got big necks.

They go in for bracelets, too, and they got a lot of arms. Legs too."

"Just who, or what are these dudes?" Bequia put in.

"They're tall," the kid put in. "And big. You don't want to meet one of them in a dark alley. Not unless you got a gun and they only got a knife."

The pirates got even more quiet.

"Did you see many guns?" Bequia asked.

"Not among the diggers, but there were some big dudes with what looked like rifles guarding the only decent building in the town. It looked to be mud brick, but it was big and guarded, kind of like a fort."

"So we ain't going to just walk in and take gold like candy from a baby," Bill pointed out.

"We got guns," came from somewhere in the crowd.

"And we ain't afraid to use 'em," followed it quickly.

The 'Yeah," "Right," "You bet," and nodding heads included even the farmers that were standing around.

Bill eyed Ben and Bequia. They all nodded together. They'd need to take every willing soul and every gun they could lay their hands on.

"Okay, folks," Bill shouted, "I'm putting it up for a vote. We've raided farmers for a few potatoes. Who's for raiding this place for gold?"

The shout was a roar.

"Anyone want to say no?"

The silence was deafening.

"Then I think we captains need to have a talk. I'm inviting every ship's captain over to my place for a drink. On me!"

That got a cheer from all.

Some of the skippers were a bit slow in moving. They were locked in talk with the leaders of their crews. No captain dared do something without the crew's hearty approval. Some had tried the "Me boss, you shit," approach and had woken up dead. Bill respected the need for those captains to talk, and only made his way slowly back to his place.

Like the hall, his captain's cabin was little more than a roof with some logs holding it up. Around here, no one did anything that wasn't open for anyone passing by to see.

Some called it the local theater, and some drama queens did provide entertainment.

Bill and his girl tried to keep it simple and fun. His crew who had put up shacks and lean-tos around his cabin said they liked it that way for their captain, seeing how he was the boss captain.

Which was to say that anyone from the hall could have followed him home and not gotten a door slammed in their face. However, with him asking them nice, none had. The captains collected around his table while Bill's girl and a couple of other women crew served the beer, whiskey, vodka, and rum.

"To rich booty," Bill shouted as he raised his mug of rum.

"To rich booty," they echoed, even some of the gals.

"Assuming we have enough guns to take it," Bequia said after taking a long pull on his whiskey.

"Yeah," came from about half the captains at the table.

"So, how do we get more guns?" Bill asked right back to them.

"We've took some from the farmers we raided," came from down the table.

"But we don't raid no farmers that got too many guns," came from further down.

"So, do we take on some better armed colonists to get

their guns?" Ben asked. "Or maybe see if some of those armed colonists aren't averse to taking some gold."

"Or do we send a ship back to Ed at LeMonte and ask him if any of his trigger-pullers might be interested in shooting some big dudes in a shooting gallery," Bill said.

That idea got some consideration.

"Do we want to share our booty with Ed and his boys and girls?" came from one of the women servers standing back from the table.

"You planning on carrying a gun in this show?" one guy captain asked, and found a small pistol expertly aimed between his eyes.

The young woman's smile was deadly. "Nobody's gonna stop me."

"No one is, pretty lady," Bill said. "Put the iron away, Dilly. You'll get your fair share, and, no doubt, a couple of guys' shares as well."

"As I'll deserve," she cooed, as the pistol disappeared under her short hem.

"Again, I ask, do we ask Ed to send us some shooters? Not anybody that ain't got a gun," Bill said.

Nobody liked sharing, but then, no one wanted to take a bite out of this goldmine only to find they'd bit off more than they could chew. After all, those dudes doing the panning were big fellows. Big and strange.

"I say we let Ed and his crew in on us taking down this planet. He can have a chunk of what we capture right then. After that, he's got to find his own goldmine," Billy finally said.

"Huzi, you take your *Ill Met By Moonlight*, and head back to LeMonte, you and Ed always was close. You tell him we want his trigger-pullers. No one else, although a light cruiser with a full 6-inch battery wouldn't be rejected if it brought a lot of rifles with it. You know what we want."

"Yeah. They pull their weight if they want any of the take."

"And tell them to be quick about it," Ben put in. "We ain't gonna sit around here forever. If they got three ships taking gold out of there, we want to get there before they get back."

"We'll get this moving," Bill assured them.

There was a knock on one of the beams that held up the roof. They'd been so concentrated on their planning that they hadn't noticed the quiet approach of Kim, who spoke for the farmers.

"You got something to say? We're kind of busy at the moment," Bill said. He got along well with Kim and his kind, but some of the pirates looked down on the kidnaped farmers no matter how much they ate the food they grew.

Bill did his best to walk a fine line.

"My people want to be included in this raid for gold."

"Kim, there will likely be fighting. People may get killed," Bill said.

"And you guys don't have no guns," Ben put in.

A very sharp knife appeared in Kim's hand. A blink of an eye later and it thudded deep into the log holding up the roof; the log the long way across from where Kim stood.

The knife had flown across most of their heads to reach its target.

Guns came out around the table.

"Put them away," Bill was saying before any of them could swing around to face the farmer.

"You think that because you found us as frozen icicles that we are defenseless. Maybe we were, fresh out of deep sleep. But we've got our muscles back, and our coordination isn't bad."

Another knife appeared in Kim's hand, "You cannot put us to work growing your bread without letting us have some sharp tools. Now, you can worry about this the next time you can't sleep, or you can make us equals in the quest for gold."

"I think you have a point," Bill said.

The table chuckled cautiously at his pun.

"Why don't you see how many of your people want to join us? See what weapons you can bring to the business, and we'll talk about this," Bill said.

He glanced around the table. He saw cautious approval and stiff-necked opposition, but those opposed to the farmers had a tendency to let their eyes wander to the knife in the roof support.

We may have to decide which we prefer. A full stomach or a good night's sleep? Or sharing the gold a bit wider.

"Ben, just how much gold is there?"

"Lots and lots of it. We saw them taking it down stream on these six legged animals. They were taking a train of twenty of them things out every other day. And the silver mine. It's a mountain, I swear to you. And they're lugging it away twenty or thirty wagon loads at a time."

"They ain't got no trucks?" a skipper asked.

"None that we seen. They was really primitive."

"So having some dirt farmers along with knives on long sticks might work out just fine in cutting their numbers down," Bill said, thoughtfully.

"Let's not cut down too many of them. I don't like the idea of having to stand knee-deep in no river panning for gold," Bequia put in.

That got a laugh.

Bill frowned at the point. They'd been treating the farmers like slaves. Now they'd just shown a surprising bit of mettle. If the pirates and the farmers let these big dudes live to work for all of them, what surprises might the farmers have in store a bit down the road?

What did grandma say? Don't count your chicks before the eggs are laid. Hell, these eggs are little more than a gleam in my eye. Be careful, Billy Boy.

7

Captain Rita Nuu-Longknife settled into the rhythms of life at Nuu House with a song in her heart. She didn't miss the hum of ship plates under foot one bit.

And little Alex did like all the attention, and a single weight, though he was growing like a well-fed weed. What with mom and dad, and Ray as well as Rita making regular pilgrimages to his nursery, he showed them all that he could take steps without them holding on to him one bit.

"He's lovely," Ray told her as they lay in bed at the end of a busy day at the ministry, which ended with a nice meal and three visits to Alex. It had been a very nice day.

"You glad to have me back?" she asked, nuzzling close.

"After last night, do you really need to ask?"

"Well, I know I have the attention of one of your heads. I was just wondering what the other one was thinking. That was one mighty gorgeous gal you brought on the *Exeter*."

Ray shook his head. "Her first comment to me was about her husband. And woman, that gal scares me. She's dangerous!"

Rita stroked his chest. "I command a heavy cruiser with twelve 8-inch lasers and you tell me you're scared of that civilian?"

Ray pulled her chin up to face him, kissed her mouth rather solidly and then said, as his lips wandered her neck, "Yes, captain, you are dangerous, but you risked your life to save mine. You're the kind of dangerous I want beside me. Her, I don't know who she is, what she's up to and I do not want her behind me. She might have a spare knife she needs to sheath between my shoulder blades."

"I've got a sheath for you," Rita purred, "and it's not between my shoulder blades."

It was a very nice night.

And in the morning, she managed to make them late for breakfast and late for work.

Andy eyed them as they walked into the outer office, and just smiled. "Good to see the two of you back and happy to be so," he said.

"I'm glad to be back," Rita said.

"You got the gallivanting out of your system?" the old Navy captain inquired of the younger.

"I think so," Rita said.

Ray lifted an eyebrow at that answer.

"I'm back. I like being back," Rita said. "But I have to tell you, it's a real high commanding my own warship. And I kind of got a kick out of chasing down all those unknowns. Come on, Ray, tell me you don't know what it's like to storm the gates of hell."

"Been there, done that. Got a medal on my chest and some metal still in my back. I keep remembering that some woman somewhere told me I'm retired."

The three of them shared a laugh at that.

"But yes," Ray continued, "I know what it's like to finish

a tough job well done. Now, from where I'm standing, we got a tough job ahead of us. A job involving too damn many meetings and memos and budgets, but a job that needs doing. Shall we?" he said, and stood aside for Rita to enter their office.

A large screen on the left wall showed the star map they'd been studying since her return. Rita glanced at it, but found nothing new jumping out at her. She noticed a new desk in the office. It was huge, easily the size of two, and had space for chairs on both sides so they could sit facing each other. One got a view of the window and the sky outside, the other got a view of the wall with the door.

"Which chair do you want?" Rita asked.

"I figure if you take the chair with the window view, you'll have a view and I'll have a view of you. We both win," Ray said. "If I take the window view, I won't know which to look at, the great view, or out the window."

She gave him a kiss for that and took the seat with her back to the window. "I like this. I've got a view and the weather outside won't distract me."

"You two are very happy to be back together, aren't you?" Andy noted.

"Very," came in two-part harmony.

"Well, I've been looking over our star map. I'd like to order the *Northampton* out for some more sniffing, likely with a pair of heavies with her."

"What did you see that I didn't?" Rita asked.

"Likely nothing, but I've been gnawing at the problem in my sleep," Andy said. "Remind me to buy some new pillows."

They chuckled at his joke.

"Anyway, it's the problem of the two jumps that take you through thick gases. I asked my computer to tell me how often you get two dirty jumps one after another. It's found thirty-five so far, but this one is the only one in our neighborhood. I know it will take a bitch of a long time, but I think the *Northampton* needs to sniff around all the jumps out of that nebula."

"They thought the sniffer lost its calibration after the nova's gas got into the intakes," Rita pointed out.

"So, we don't activate the sniffer until we're out of the gas clouds. Someone has to be able to come up with a cap or seal or something to cover over the intake."

"Right," again came in a duet.

"I'll get the Navy yard on the job," Ray said. "We'll want to pick a pair of heavies and have them ready when Matt's boat is out of the body and fender shop."

"That should be in a week," Rita said. Keeping a heavy cruiser shipshape and battle-ready was more of a job than she'd had with her transports, but then, there was a whole lot more that could go wrong and when you're prowling around looking for wreckage, you're risking having someone not like what you just nosed into. That is not time for something to go wrong."

"I think we can make that happen. A week won't be that long," Ray said. "And we've got other ships out cruising the spaceways, just begging to be scooped up by some bold pirate man."

"I don't know if we'll get any bites," Andy said. "It's been a while."

"I got one," Rita said.

"Yeah," Ray said, "but you are so desirable."

"I'll leave you two love birds to do whatever it is you're up to," Andy said, and headed back to his office.

The morning went fast. They managed to go home for lunch, both so Rita could feed Alex and they could squeeze in a quickie. Still, by one, she was back at the ministry and Ray was over with Admiral Zilko.

Which put Ray in a very happy mood on the drive home. "Your father, or someone got the government to cut loose more money. We not only have enough to crew another three ships, but a contract has been signed with Savannah to build six heavy cruisers and pay for them to outfit another half-dozen scouts that are being collected from the mothball fleets around our side of the rim."

"You think your dangerous civilian had her lovely manicured fingers in this?" Rita asked.

"What have you got against her?"

"She's gorgeous, and flaunts it . . . near my husband."

Ray leaned over and kissed her. "But said husband only has eyes for you."

"But a girl can worry, can't she?"

"She can worry all she wants, so long as she does it right here beside me."

"Always," Rita said.

Or at least for the next couple of weeks. Or months. Maybe we can both ship out on the Exeter. Alex will be weaned soon. He wouldn't miss us if we were gone for just the few weeks it would take to clean out a pirate nest.

We'll have the time we need to make it all come together.

8

C aptain Edmon Lehrer, the closest thing to a commander the proud pirate base LeMonte had, was surprised at how quickly the pirates made it all came together. Usually you had to make every decision three or four times because someone didn't like it or wanted to go over it again.

Of course, if you even whisper the word "gold" around people like his crew, they were running before you finish the word.

That they had no idea who or what those big fellows were digging out the gold, much less how much of a fight they might put up seemed to worry very few.

Ed spent several hours in counsel with that few.

"They're trying to have us buy a pig in a poke." Grace O'Malley of the *Happy Highway Wench* was one of the doubters. Not that she wasn't one of the best at taking a colony for every last scrap of bacon and drop of beer when they raided one at the rim of human space.

"We could look things over before we charge in," Anne Bonney of the *Proper Daughter's Revenge*, said.

"I agree," Calico Jack said, nodding. He often agreed with the ladies and rarely left meetings alone. Ed had his doubt about his value in council, but he was a veteran of the Unity War and the best ground fighter they had. Half the guns in the armory had been taken when he chose to face down a bunch of colonists on Cle Elum.

For a while it had looked like it would come to a bloody fight, but Calico Jack had managed to maneuver his troops between the amateur army the farmers had thrown together and the nearest water supply. Confronted with having to attack entrenched riflemen to fill their canteens, common sense prevailed.

Jack had agreed to reduce his demands by half, and the Cle Elum's jumped up colonel had agreed to surrender half his rifles with the other half put well aside. The colonials had promised Jack fervently that they'd have more guns coming on the next ship and then they'd be only too glad to offer him a rematch.

Jack had managed to make off with not only the half of the armory they'd surrendered, but got his hands on the rest of their guns on the way out. Still, no pirate had been back to Cle Elum since.

So Calico Jack's crew was the best armed, right ahead of Grace O'Malley and Anne Bonney's crew. Exactly what the gals traded for rifles was something Ed was only too happy to speculate on.

"You aren't going to put us under that Billy Maynard?" Grace said. "The man's a fool and a hot head, when he's not being led around by his gonads."

"I do agree that we need to keep our own chain of command," Calico Jack said. "We'll do what you and him agree on, but we do it our way."

"That is my plan," Ed said. "I'll coordinate with Bill, but I won't have you doing anything I don't think is good for us."

"How's the loot going to be shared?" Calico Jack asked.

"That's a sticking point, but not one that should delay us. Of what we get for actually laying our crews on the line, twenty-five percent of what we capture in the first week will be split evenly between the captains. Thirty percent goes to the sailors that stay in orbit. The rest, forty-five percent goes to those that land with a gunner getting double what a non-gunner gets."

"Non-gunner?" Calico Jack asked.

"Some of the farm hands at Port Elgin want in on the landing action. They'll have knives, spears, whatever is steel and has a sharp edge."

"They're gonna get clobbered if there's any serious fighting," Grace said.

Ed shrugged. "Their report says that these jokers are mostly miners what don't have any weapons. And there are a lot of them. We'll likely need more people covering the prisoners than we got rifles so it's not such a bad idea. Still, as they said, gunners get double the pay of knife men."

"Or women," Anne said.

"Yeah," Ed agreed. "Anyway, we'll know more when we got everyone out there and are looking the place over from orbit. That's when we'll decide how it comes down."

"What if they got ships in orbit?" Grace O'Malley asked.

"Then we either cut and run or we stand and fight. I'm taking the *Queen Anne's Revenge*. Black Bart will have the *Your Bad Day*. We've got twelve working 6-inchers between us. My crew's working hard on getting that last 6-inch back on line. Your ships between them add in another half dozen 6-inchers and an equal number of 4-inchers."

Ed eyed the captains. They nodded agreement. Hopefully no more lasers would get sick, lame or lazy before they could carry off this raid. If they really did get gold out of this, they might be able to bribe some more salvage yards to give them parts, or even a cruiser or two.

Everything depended on getting the gold.

"What's Billy boy got at, what's that place, Port Elgin?" Grace asked.

"Yeah, Port Elgin. When he left here, he took half of what we had," Ed said. "Depending on what of his has come down with the dropsy, he could double our force, or maybe not."

"This Captain Huzi tell you anything about what they got?"

"Nothing I believe," Ed said. His old granny had told him not to ask a question he didn't want the answer to or trust the answer he got. Huzi was all grand talk. Ed was still trying to figure out how much of it to believe.

Ed trusted him for the sack of gold nuggets he'd dropped on the table . . . and not a farthing more.

"Well, we're wasting time," O'Malley said, coming to her feet. "I figure I can get the *Wench* away from the pier by this time tomorrow."

"The *Revenge* will be right behind you," Anne said.

"And the *Queen Anne's Revenge* will be at the head of your line," Ed said.

"Does that mean my *You Didn't See This Coming* and *Your Worst Nightmare* have to come up the rear?" Calico Jack said with a laughing whine.

"You never minded coming up my rear," O'Malley said.

"But your front was the *goal*. Now your rear will be between me and the *gold*."

"Doesn't he say the nicest things?" Anne said.

"That's the only reason we keep him around," O'Malley said.

"And I thought it was because I shoot so nice and straight."

"Get over yourself, boy."

"Or over you?"

"Not tonight. If I'm getting this show on the road, I got some lasers to babysit, parts to scavenge, and heads to knock," Grace said.

"Business before pleasure, boy. Business before pleasure. Remember that," Annie said.

"I think they got that right," Ed said.

"Yeah. This time tomorrow," Calico Jack said.

Captain Edmon Lehrer didn't know whether to be surprised or shocked, but by that time the next day, he was indeed leading ten ships away from the pier right behind his *Revenge* as they all headed for the furthest jump point.

They weren't all just eager pirates. Some of his farmers had produced some wicked looking blades, tightly wound to long stout wooden poles, and demanded to be taken along.

The two usual hanger queens were still tied up alongside. The *Sengo* and the *Yaka* had been in pretty poor shape when they were taken, and had been more a source of parts than real ships since arriving at LeMonte. They'd managed to struggle away from the yard at High Savannah loaded with machinery of questionable worth and men, former soldiers, and cops of even more questionable value.

Except for them, and the worse drunks and dregs as well as the more docile farmers, everyone was headed out for gold and glory.

Assuming they could trust any word they got from Port Elgin.

9

Major General Ray Longknife didn't know whether to be glad or mad. He had a lot to be glad for, but he had a damn itch he could not scratch and that was driving him up the walls.

He tried to focus on what he had to be grateful for.

Rita was home. She was in his bed every night and he woke up beside her every morning. He understood that many men found that to be a most fulfilling existence.

No question, it was nice.

He had a growing boy. He had the cutest little grin with the cutest tiny teeth, and he was taking his first steps, usually from his mommy's loving arms to his daddy's outstretched hands.

Oh, and his first words were "da da."

Ray kept trying to tell himself this was a wonderful life.

And Ray was training a division of troops. The proud 2nd brigade was now just one of three brigades under his command. And Earth had made it official. They were the 1st Wardhaven Division, Society of Humanity Army, under the command of a Society of Humanity major general.

There had even been a big ceremony where Rita had pinned on his second star.

"But don't forget," she'd whispered in his ear. "You're still retired."

Well, for someone retired, he was spending a lot of time at the cantonment outside Wardhaven seeing that the troops were properly trained. The politicians that dropped by to watch them parade or maneuver too often mumbled, "It's only pirates you'll be going up against, Right?'"

Ray had gotten a hold of some video taken on a planet named Cle Elum where there had damn near been a major force engagement with regimental size battle groups on both sides. The colonials had not even had mortars in support. The pirates had managed to knock together a couple of them, and that, along with the savvy way the pirate commander outfoxed the locals on their own ground and got between them and water, had settled the matter.

The locals were drilling a lot more now and had bought mortars, support rockets, and artillery. Ray made a point of talking up the quality of the Cle Elum militia when he talked to his junior officer's mess.

"If you can't get your shit together, I'll damn well hire up some of the Cle Elum militia."

His troops trained hard.

So, three days a week, maybe four, he was out at the cantonment. Two days a week, sometimes one, he was back at the ministry.

Still, every night, he was home with Rita, and the compromise seemed to satisfy her.

However, if Ray was reading the smoke signals right, his woman was itching in places neither she nor he could scratch.

"Damn," was the first word out of her mouth when he picked her up one afternoon on his way home.

"Bad day at the office?"

"We've got a message back from the *Northampton*. She's checked out the jumps from that nebula that she didn't go over because of her messed-up sniffer last time."

"And she found . . ." Ray said, knowing that both of them wanted her to say Matt had found the trail of the pirates, but he suspected the initial "Damn" meant he hadn't.

"Nothing. Oh, they got some jumps that had more residual reaction mass in the vacuum of space than other jumps, but there wasn't enough to make a definite trail. They'd have to chase down one after another of the jumps, check them all out, and they could be doing that from now until doomsday."

"Does Matt have any suggestion as to why the trail's gone cold?"

"Either they've got several paths in and out of human space," Rita said, "or the trail is cold because they haven't used it for a while."

"Maybe I've had my head in too much mean green," Ray said, "but have the raiding depredations slowed down?"

"They most certainly have, my general. We've got more buoys out now. We're having them jump through at least once a day. That makes for more communication out on the rim and lets us know if we've lost a buoy sometime during the day. Anyway, it's been a couple of weeks since any colony got hit with independent tax collectors, as they have taken to calling themselves."

"We ought to wipe them out if for no other reason than their lousy sense of humor," Ray said.

"Well, I'm wondering if they're going into a second

phase. No, third phase. Chasing ships. Raiding colonies. Now, what?"

"Could their crops be coming in? Maybe they have enough to eat and don't need to raid planets for food."

"Yes, but what are they *doing*? Sitting on their asses, twiddling their thumbs?"

Ray made a face at that thought. "Pirates don't usually choose a line of work that lets them live long and retire comfortably. They want all that glitters. Where are they getting it? Whitebred? We burned out Milassi's drug farm, but he said he saved some seeds. Could they be going into the drug business?"

"I wondered about that, but there are no reports of a sudden influx of new drugs. The usual stuff, but nothing special. I even chased down some of the scientists that worked on the drug farm that Ruth and your Mary burned out on Savannah. It didn't take much to get them talking about what they were trying to grow. I ran that through channels and nobody has seen anything like it coming to market."

Ray made a sour face. "All we're getting is negatives. They haven't done this. They aren't doing that. What are they doing?"

"I just don't know, love, and I don't like that."

"Neither do I," Ray said.

"Well, we're home. Forget the job and let's see what new things Alex did today."

Ray tried to. He really did. But it was hard looking at one tiny fellow's efforts to stay up for four steps while you wondered how some pirate bastard was staying a whole lot of steps ahead of them.

10

———

Captain Edmon Lehrer led the *Queen Anne's Revenge* into the target system. There were two of those strange ball ships in orbit around their target planet. They took off running as soon as they saw the pirate fleet.

They might have gotten away.

But just as they were a few hundred thousand clicks from the other jump point out of the system, they ran right into Captain Billy Maynard's fleet coming in. The round ships had too much momentum; there was no way for them to get enough energy on their boats to turn a deceleration towards the jump into an acceleration away from it.

Billy's ships cut them to ribbons. Then, most of them accelerated toward the golden planet, leaving a couple of ships behind to sift through the wreckage.

It was just as they all expected, the ships they'd cut up with their lasers were loaded with gold, silver, jewelry quality diamonds and other gemstones, all there for the taking.

It just kept getting better and better.

Captain Maynard squawked, but Calico Jack commanded the landing force for the very simple reason that two out of every three trigger-pullers were his, or Grace's and Annie's and the three of them insisted their troops would only follow Jack.

That led to some rather delightful if tasteless innuendoes. Calico Jack enjoyed them all, since he was just as happy with a pretty young thing of either persuasion in his bed and made no bones about it.

They chose a nice, sandy beach about five miles around the bay from what they took for the main, if only town. The first shuttles dropped with half their gunners aboard.

Once the shuttles were beached and the troops ashore, Calico Jack ordered his trigger-pullers to dig in.

"We didn't come down here to dig. That's what we got those guys for," came from one of Billy Maynard's proud boys with a rifle.

Calico knocked the guy for a loop, snatched up his gun and pointed it at the fool. "Dig you bastards, dig! I don't care what you came here for, you'll dig when I say so, and where I say so. Now get some blisters on those lily-white hands."

They dug.

The second drop brought more gunners. Only the later drops brought the spear and knife crew. To some obnoxious trigger-puller's great disappointment, the digging was all done by the time the farmers arrived with their bladed weapons.

That was a good thing, because the big dudes with all the arms and legs didn't wait to be attacked but moved out on their own. And it wasn't a dumb attack they made.

Ed's *Revenge* was passing overhead when the attack developed.

"You need any help?" he asked Calico Jack on net.

"This guy is a lot smarter than I wish he was, and his troops are a lot more disciplined than I really want to face. Maybe more disciplined than the jokers I've got behind me. And on top of that, there are a lot more of them than I was expecting. Would you mind lazing the trees off on my right? He's trying to envelope my right wing and I'd prefer if he didn't."

One of *Revenge's* 6-inch lasers cut into tree looking things four kilometers off of the beach.

"You got the right area, but you're about half a klick too far from the beach. Bring it in. Shave the hair off my butt."

"If you say so."

A second 6-inch laser set trees burning closer to the beach.

"You got it," Calico shouted. "Now hammer him."

Salvo after salvo sliced into the trees, turning them into a burning inferno visible from even two hundred kilometers up.

"Glad I'm a sailor," Ed's second in command muttered as she watched the screen.

"I'm glad you are too," he told his lover.

"Just make sure we get paid. I want to wear nothing but gold coins to bed, like you promised.

"Just keep your focus here for now," Ed said. Around him, his crew heard him and applied themselves to the day's work.

On the ground, the aliens broke and fell back. Jack's call for some more shoots were answered by Grace or Annie, or whatever ship happened to be in his sky at the time of the call.

Not all ships were created equal. Jack called off a shoot by Ben Hornigold's ship when the jerk made a mess of it for some of his own landing party.

"That's going to cost you," Ed snapped. "Cost you gold. Billy, did you see that?"

"I'm on the other side of the damn planet or I'd have been doing the shooting," the co-commander of the fleet growled. "Ben, keep your guns to yourself and we'll talk about what cut we take out of your share when this is done."

"He didn't give me a good call," Ben Hornigold insisted. "They're running and you're chasing them real fast down there. You listen in on the net calls. I shot where I was told to."

"We settle this later."

The next time Ed was above the town, there were humans moving through the streets. There were also the big dudes. The high res cameras showed a lot of them with their hands up, surrendering.

The ground troops were letting them. Someone had to mine the gold and it sure wasn't going to be pirates.

Slavery, here we come, Ed thought.

They hadn't treated their own farmers as slaves, and from the looks of those sharp things those plow boys had tied to poles, it was a good thing they hadn't.

Ed studied the pictures coming in of the big dudes and wondered how they'd take to being told to do all the scut work. No doubt they didn't talk good standard. Maybe if they learned it, some of the more gutsy types could be signed on as pirates. Heaven knew, humans worked better if they saw a chance to work the way up the food chain.

Not all of the big dudes were terribly eager to put their hands up. One building in the middle of town kept shooting. It was big and blocky, made from mud bricks with, apparently, thick walls.

Calico Jack settled its hash with his mortars. He dropped explosive bombs mixed with smoke grenades, covering for men to slip in and slap explosive charges on the massive wooden doors. One good explosion and the door was down, the portal was open, and gunners were running in.

Ed Lehrer wasn't above the town when the fort fell, but what Calico found was beamed around the orbiting ships. "We've got the treasure house here. Gold. Silver piled to the ceiling, and jewels fit to swim in, I shit you not."

That produced a lot of happy talk aboard the orbiting ships. Not doubt on the ground as well.

The cleaning up process got started before the afternoon was half gone. Now the shuttles dropped with solar-powered runabouts. They were quickly rigged with machine guns and a couple of companies of eager pirates raced up to the silver mine.

They didn't find a lot there.

Somehow, word had gotten up into the mine of the new gun in town; the workers had taken to the hills. A check of what looked like food stores showed them empty except for some crates full of something that looked like yams. Others held seaweed.

"They'll come in when they get hungry enough," Calico Jack said, then he began issuing orders. "Set up your perimeter, dig in for the night, and see that you post a watch. Two hours on, six off, through the night."

While the race for the mine had been going on, mixed troops of guns and pikes headed up the river to collect those panning for gold. Most were eager to put their hands up, what with a gun in their face, and, once collected, they were marched back to town.

A former top sergeant from Savannah pushed on, way up-river with a force of about a hundred rifles and an equal number of pikes. Nightfall caught him with some five hundred big aliens way too far from town. He used ropes to tie them up to trees and let his own troops sleep, without posting a watch or guard.

How it happened, no one was left to tell the tale, but come morning, that entire detachment, two hundred strong, was found dead in their sleeping rolls with their throats slit.

"I don't think this is going to be as easy as some people thought. Not if we're going to do stupid stuff like that," Calico Jack was heard to mutter the next day when a scout he sent out to check on the silence from up river answered him with bloody pictures on the net.

The pirates, both those with guns and those with pole weapons, were a lot more careful the next morning as they herded several hundred of the big fellows out to pan for gold in the river close to the town. They didn't find a lot.

"It looks like they panned out the river right close to town," Calico Jack reported that evening.

"So, what are we going to do?" Ed Maynard demanded on the ship's net.

"We'll head the big fellows up the river, with plenty of guards, and knock together forts along the river," Calico Jack said, bluntly. "Today, we walk them up. They can dig a couple of ditches and wall forts. We'll guard them at night," he said forcefully, eyes on someone off screen, "and we'll bring in the gold every couple of days."

"That sounds like a plan," Ed said. Billy nodded.

"Well, I got my own plan," Ben Hornigold growled. "Me and mine aren't interested in wallowing around in the mud. Ben says some ships took off with the gold before he could catch them. I'm gonna go looking for where they took it. There's more than one way to take candy from a baby."

"You sure they're all babies?" Ed said, cautiously. He eyed Grace and Anne. They shook their heads, but not enough to be noticed by Ben.

"We took them down here, didn't we?" Ben Hornigold growled.

"And we have a lot of dead pirates down here now," Calico Jack said.

"As I said, you can play patty-cakes in the mud," Ben said snidely. "I'll go get me some ships and gold."

Ben Hornigold and Black Bart departed as soon as they could recover their riflemen from the planet. Ed didn't really feel they were much of a loss.

Just how big a loss they were would only become clear later.

11

Captain Rita Nuu-Longknife, Co-Minister of Exploration for Wardhaven, was getting bored. She was doing a job, pushing paperwork from the in-basket to the out-basket. She was doing good work, getting ships out to make the space ways safe for commerce.

She knew that.

Still, nothing was happening.

Really, *nothing* was happening.

The raids on the more distant colonies had stopped. Possibly it was because the distant colonies had armed themselves.

"It's amazing what a couple of 81-mm mortars will do to a pirate raid," her husband, Major General Ray Longknife, muttered on the drive home that evening.

"I wouldn't mind if those mortars did something to the pirates. I'd *love* to see some pictures of what they did to the pirates," Rita said.

"No you wouldn't, love. What mortars leave behind is not pretty."

"Excuse me, honey. I'm the transport pilot, remember. I left the rough stuff to you and your guard brigade."

"Don't fool me, love, you stayed behind to pick up the pieces. At least the pieces of me."

That got Rita a kiss she knew she had earned the hard way.

"You know what I really mean. We had a pirate problem. We walked on hot coals to get people to fund some anti-pirate work. Now, we've got ships in space and troop assistance teams out there on the ground and, *voila*, no pirates."

"Yeah, that bothers me, too," Ray said.

"So, what are we going to do about it?"

Ray Longknife pondered her question long and hard. He didn't have an answer that night, or the next morning.

That morning was Friday. It was the one day she could count on Ray to spend at the office, not out with his 1st Ward-haven Guard Division doing whatever strong men armed did when there wasn't anything to blow up.

So, the two of them found themselves staring at the star map that covered one whole long wall in their Exploration office.

"Has anything changed?" Ray asked, eyeing the map of planets plundered, freighters gone missing on the normal space lanes and exploration ships just gone somewhere out along their scouting sweeps.

"For a month, it's been the same," Rita said, "at least as far as it goes within human space. We've got another two overdue explorers."

"Cruisers?" Ray asked.

"Nope. I've got our Rambling class cruisers feeling around the rim, but not too far out. It's the privately funded scout ships. It's two ten-place schooners that are overdue and maybe missing."

"Unarmed?"

"Not so much as a .45 among the crew, I'm led to believe."

"You believe them."

"Not on your life, but there's no way to put even a 3-inch pop gun on something that small."

"Assuming it's actually something that small," Ray rumbled.

"You don't trust the private folks any further than you can throw them?"

"Less," Ray said. "There's too much money to be made in exploration, honey. If they find a new Earth, they can sell it by the pound."

Rita highlighted the two new missing ships. All the deep exploration ships that hadn't come back formed a red cloud. It was a thin cloud, but it clearly covered the quarter of the rim of human space on Wardhaven's side.

"Is it my imagination, but isn't Savannah about in the center of the rim where we're bleeding scouts?"

Rita nodded.

Ray walked slowly up to the map, fingered the space around the rim that bled red.

"You want to go back to Savannah?" Rita asked.

Ray nodded. "Somewhere out there are aliens. Worse, somewhere out there are human pirates. I really wish I could ditch the fear in the pit of my stomach that the two of them aren't separate and distinct problems anymore."

"It's not just your stomach, love."

"You too, honey?"

"Me too."

"Any suggestion?"

"I'm thinking my mother wasn't nearly as bad a mother as I thought she was a few years ago. I'm thinking that I might want to leave little Alex with her for a bit while you and I run the *Exeter* over to Savannah to see how things are going there."

Ray nodded. "Because if we have to throw together a Rapid Reaction Force, it's likely going to be heading out from there. If it's not, it's just going to be a slow reaction force that gets there too little and too late."

They nodded. Rita turned to check on the availability of the *Exeter*. Ray did his own call to the 1st Guard. With luck, he should be able to pull a company out of the training cycle and load them aboard Rita's ship.

Maybe if she could lay her hands on four ships, he could take an entire battalion.

12

C aptain Edmon Lehrer tried to keep his cruisers as fully crewed as possible. He was none too sure what lay beyond the jumps into this system and he was not at all happy to have Ben Hornigold and Black Bart charging around beyond his ken.

However, you can only keep a crew in zero gee so long before they start to lose important things. Like bones and muscle mass. Even eyesight gets off. Not good for a gunner.

Every day, he let a quarter of his crew go below for two days. Six days up. Two days down. If he had to push it, the shuttles could get the ships fully crewed in six, maybe nine hours. It would be pushing it, but it could be done.

Any ship coming through the three jump points into the system would take a lot more than twelve hours to get here even if they were pushing two gees.

It seemed like a safe way to run things.

Of course, once ashore, the crew had to have something to do.

And that was where the rub came in.

The most profitable thing to do was pan for gold. Lots of

sailors thought it would be fun to try their hand at it. Any gold they took out themselves was theirs to keep, no requirement to share it with the others, or even the captains.

So, when it was Ed's time to go down, he decided to take a try at it. Of course, the river near town was all worked out, so he got Calico Jack to drive him up to the fourth fort up river.

It seemed like such a good idea at the time.

The day was clear, as most had been since they landed. The drive was a bit rugged. "They didn't bother to make any decent roads up here," Calico said from his place behind the wheel. "They used pack animals to get food up river and gold down."

If the drive was rough, the scenery was beautiful. Beside them, a fifty-meter-wide river flowed placidly over rocks and gravel. It was clean, in most places, though where a lot of the big fellows were panning, it got a bit murky.

On both sides of the river, the jungle came down to the river, except where it had been hacked back. There were flashes of just about every color along with the green.

"What's that like?" Ed said, nodding at the color splotched green.

"You don't want to go there," Calico said, giving it a cautious eye. "They got stuff in there with leaves as sharp as steel. I swear to God, I think some of it cuts you and enjoys the taste of your blood."

"Really?"

"I can't really know anything about this place, but from the eager way it slashes at you if you walk in there, I'd sure say the damn plants are doing it for some reason."

Ed was sitting in the passenger seat, close to the jungle. He edged away from the doorless chassis.

The fort was about what he'd expected from his view in

orbit. The jungle had been slashed back from a flat bit of alluvial gravel. The dirt, rocks and gravel from the ditch had been thrown up into a four-sided walled enclosure. Inside were pens for the big fellows and tents for the humans. At least at this fort, guards with guns and pikes walked the walls, eyes both in and out.

Ed felt safe as he and his number two tucked themselves into their bedrolls, enjoyed each other's gifts and drifted off to sleep to the sound of night calls from the jungle.

Until he woke up the next morning to a woman screaming.

Ed and Number Two were out of their bedrolls in a flash. Pistols in hand, if nothing else on, they raced to the next tent. There, a guy lay next to the shrieking woman.

He grinned through an entirely new smile halfway down his throat.

"Damn it, how could anything that big get in unnoticed last night?" was the unanswered question posed to no one by Calico Jack as he joined them, his night's companion at his side, also naked, but with a rifle in her hands.

Ed scowled at Calico.

"You didn't mention that these big fellows could get around that quietly."

"This is the first time it's happened in a guarded fort."

"If they'd picked the next tent over, that could have been me," Ed said, suddenly feeling a lot more vulnerable than just from the insect-like things buzzing his naked skin.

A couple of shots rang out.

Ed and Calico looked at each other.

Then several assault rifles went to full rock and roll.

"Oh, shit," Calico whispered, and as one, the four of them turned back to the open commons.

It was a bloody mess. Big fellows lay everywhere. Some

dead. Others moaning and trying to drag their large bodies away from the slaughter.

"What the hell happened here?" Calico demanded.

No one said anything.

"Something happened here," Calico shouted. "Somebody better start talking or I'll take my knife to the lot of you."

"Th . . . that . . . that one tried to run," a young gunner stammered. Ed recognized him. He was from the *Queen Anne's Revenge.* He'd come down on the same shuttle with Ed.

Where'd he get the gun?

"I was told to stand watch," the kid said, explaining how a sailor had ended up with a gun. "That one didn't stop when I shouted 'halt.' He just kept going. He was trying to escape."

"That one?" Calico said, pointing at one very dead big one. "The one next to the food box?"

"That's a food box?" The kid's eyes got wide, but at least his rifle was now pointed at the ground.

"Yeah. It took us a couple of days to realize they ate that crap," Calico Jack said. "I don't think they really like it," he told Ed. "But when they're hungry enough, they eat those kinds of yams. Yes, kid, he was going for his one meal of the day."

The kid was turning whiter shades of white. He dropped his gun, barrel down, into the mud.

"Okay, that says why one of them got dead. How come they all are?"

"They charged the wall," a middle-aged woman said, her gun carried easily by its sling around her neck. "They all charged the wall. It was kill them or have them go over. I guess they panicked."

"And maybe we did too," Calico said, eyeing all the trigger-pullers with smoking guns. "How many of you just got down here last night?"

All but two or three raised their hands.

"Maggie?" Calico said, raising his voice.

The middle-aged woman shrugged, but kept her gun pointed at no one ... and all of them.

"The troops down here needed a good night sleep, so I put the new kids on the watch. Hell, Jack, in a day or two they can go back up to orbit and enjoy some rest. Us down here aren't getting a lot of sleep."

"Damn," Calico Jack muttered. "Maggie, you put a bunch of dumb shits on the watch. No wonder we got this."

"You didn't tell me not to."

"I didn't say that you could."

Again, Maggie shrugged. "So, what do we do with the bodies?"

Calico grimaced. "Make sure they're all bodies. Then pile them up and burn them. We can't have the ones at the other forts knowing about this. And hell, we can't have the ones in the jungle any the wiser, either."

There was a whistling sound. Ed looked up to see a huge rock sailing through the sky. He gauged its flight, and stood his ground.

It smashed into a tent. There was a brief scream from someone who'd managed to sleep through the morning's racket. A very brief scream that quickly died with finality.

"Where'd that come from?" Ed demanded, and then moved aside. A second one tumbled to the ground where he'd been standing, bounced, and rolled into the tent with the slit throat.

A woman screamed and others ran to help her. She had

to be dragged out. Her leg was twisted in a way no leg should be.

"Get her to the medic," Calico ordered. "And watch your heads!" he added tersely as another rock slammed into a now empty tent. Everyone was up now.

"Where are these damn rocks coming from?" Ed demanded.

"Damned if I know," was Calico's only answer.

"*Revenge*, come in," Ed said to his commlink.

"Number Three here, boss," came in an eager voice.

"You know what fort I'm at?"

"I got you located, boss. We're overhead. Sorry I can't beam you up."

"Bad joke, Number Three. Someone in the jungle is tossing rocks at us. Can you spot them?"

"Give us a minute, boss. Yeah, that's your grinning face. Boss, you should have washed up. You got something in your teeth."

"Worse joke. Tell me you got who's tossing rocks at us."

"Oh, watch out. One's coming in."

Ed looked up. The rock wasn't headed anywhere close to him, but across the square, several gunners and pikes made space for it.

"Yep, I got them. Stupid looking thing, boss. They're using ropes to pull at trees."

"Laze them."

"Give me a minute, boss. It ain't like we're not playing with ourselves while the cat's away."

"Laze them," Ed repeated.

Off in the distance, the air got hazy and, suddenly, there was an explosion and trees flying every which way and a fire breaking out.

"There's more of them, boss."

"Hit 'em," Calico Jack said over Ed's shoulder.

"Do it," Ed said.

"Doing it, boss," and another explosion and more flying trees and fire.

They didn't have to ask for the third or fourth shot.

"I think that's all of them. At least that we can make out from here," Number Three reported.

"Good job. Advise the next ships in orbit what you did. Things are changing down here."

"It sure looks like it."

Ed turned to Calico Jack and raised a questioning eyebrow. Jack turned to Maggie. "Get your best troops together and get out there and clean up this mess. I want to know how they're throwing rocks around."

"I'll get right on it, Jack," she said, and turned to several hard-looking gun types. "Get the maggots out of bed, and sober or not, we're going for a walk in the jungle."

"Not that place," came from one, but she was already turning to shout orders to a couple of others who rounded up more gunners and pikes and got them moving toward the gate.

"What do we do?" the space pirate who'd started the whole mess asked plaintively.

"Well, you can get all your fellow tourists," Calico Jack said, "pile these bodies up and burn them. Then, if you have any time left, you can pan for gold, though I'd suggest that at least half of you keep your guns up and eyes on the jungle. Mind you, I'm not telling you to, but I'd strongly suggest it."

Calico was as aware as Ed that pirates didn't take orders well. Today, it looked like Jack's suggestion was carrying the power of law. Those not forming up to assault the jungle turned to, piling up big bodies and hunting up gas to start the fire.

Once they torched the pile, the stink was enough to drive everyone out of the fort. Even those headed into the jungle with the bloodthirsty leaves seemed relieved to get away from the stink.

"What do we do?" Ed asked Jack.

"We, me bucko, get our tired asses back into town. If they can toss rocks in daylight and sneak into camp to slit throats at night, I think we need to rethink our priorities. Mind you, I'm not telling all you other captains what to do, but if we aren't willing to look to our own defenses before gold digging, I'm getting my ass and all the asses following me the hell out of this place."

"You'll be behind me," Ed said.

Calico Jack organized a well-armed convoy. Ed's Number Two gave him a quick kiss and headed for one of the gun trucks. She slapped in a 500-round magazine, pulled the arming bolt back on the machine gun, and set an intent look on her face.

She was very good in bed, but she did like blowing shit up.

The drive down river was only slightly faster, though a whole lot bumpier.

As they approached the third fort, they came across three gunners lounging on the bank and a dozen big fellows wading in the river shallows, panning. The gunners took one look at the convoy and stood up.

One of them approached Calico Jack. "You look like death on a stick, if you don't mind me saying so, Captain."

"We've had trouble up river," Jack said.

"We heard the explosions. Saw the fires."

"Then you should have known to be more alert," Calico said.

"A fellow can't stay on his toes all the time."

"Now might be a good time to see how long you can."

The gunner eyed Calico, then glanced up river where the smoke was still billowing. He turned back to his mates. "Okay, crew, let's keep alert. Just cause yesterday was boring don't mean today will be."

The other two eyed the convoy, then the smoke, then one of them turned to search the jungle not five meters from them. The other eyed the big fellows. Some of them had noticed the smoke. No doubt they'd heard the explosions if the gunners had.

One of them waded a bit deeper out into the river. Dug up a pan full of gravel, sluiced it about a few times, then galloped for deeper water and dove.

The big fellow didn't make it. A machine gun cut him near in half. Ed looked back to see Number Two grinning over her sights.

"I knew that one was going to make a go for it," she said.

"You got him good," the senior local gunner said.

"You better get the next one," Calico Jack said. "We're heading east," and so saying, gunned his rig onward.

The crew they talked with must have had a commlink. When they got to the third fort, its walls were already manned with alert guards, walking the ramparts. Others were moving out to reinforce the guards watching the aliens pan for gold. Even some of the sailors that had come down to do their own panning were being handed guns or pikes and seemed to be taking them on with a will.

It was noon as they rolled into town. The impact of the morning had arrived ahead of them. Guards were out, overseeing big ones hacking back the jungle. Others were digging out a moat and building up a wall. No doubt, the shooters on that wall would have clear fire lanes.

Calico Jack took them right up to what they'd identified as the governor's palace, next to the fortified treasure house. Made of mud brick like the treasure house, it had a high ceiling made of long tree trunks. It was divided up into several smaller rooms around one great room with a long plank table. There were three-legged stools around it. Jack considered it the governor's palace because it was large and mud brick with lots of gold and silver plate lining the walls. Of computer terminals or comm stations, there wasn't one in sight. Interesting.

Several captains were already waiting for them.

"What happened?" "What's going on?" "How bad is it?" were only a few of the questions that greeted them.

"Come inside and we'll talk about it," Calico said, and stormed in the door, through the hall and into the vast meeting room. He knew just where the liquor locker was and had it open and a bottle of rum in his hands in no time. Only when it was half empty did he turn to those behind him.

"Take a seat. This is going to be a long meeting," Calico Jack said, and the captains did as he suggested.

"We got problems," he said, and told them of his morning. "Ed was up there with me. It was his *Revenge* that blew their little jungle sling shots to hell."

Captain Edmon Leher nodded in affirmation of the story.

"How could one of those big lugs tiptoe into one of our forts at night with guards out?" Captain Huzi demanded.

"Was it one of them or one of us?" asked Grace O'Malley, who'd just come down for some R&R.

"Good question," Ed said. "It kind of got exciting around

the old fort after that, so I can't say that we really did much of a job investigating the little knifing. Still, the gal in the bedroll next to the guy seemed to be truly put off by the whole affair. It didn't exactly look like she did it herself."

"But how didn't she know the guy next to her was being knifed?" Huzi shot right back at Ed.

"Ladies and gentlemen," Calico Jack said, "I don't rightly care whether she knifed him or he knifed himself, the problem is those big fellows out there. The ones we have aren't nearly as docile as they've been making out to be. One tried to run already this morning and got shot down."

"He's not the only one," Grace said. "We've had several reports back this morning of runners. Those explosions up your way, Jack, could be heard all the way down here. They may not have been as loud as they were there, but we heard them. And if my eyes aren't lying to me, the big fellows are whispering among themselves a lot."

"Can't we stop that?" Billy Maynard asked. "Shoot any that does?"

"That would be all of them," Grace said, dryly.

"Maybe we need to shoot them all," came from somewhere down the table. Ed didn't see who it was that tossed that ugly dog on the table, but once there, it just laid there. No one said yes and no one said no to the proposition.

"You want to do all the sweating to get the gold out of that damn river? We're getting nothing out of that mountain of silver up there. Not a damn thing," Billy pointed out. "And as for where they got the jewels, nobody seems to have any idea. We're sitting on a fortune and it's just laying out there in the mud."

That did get a lot of grumbling agreement.

Calico Jack's commlink buzzed at that moment. "Yes," he

snapped. The rum seemed to be having its effect. Jack was a nasty, roaring drunk.

"Maggie here, boss. We've found what was tossing the rocks in the fort."

"What was it? They build a catapult or something?" Jack asked.

"No. It looks like this damn place grows them."

"Huh?"

"There's this tree. It's one long trunk with some nasty stuff on the top, but it bends in the wind a lot and that's how it tosses its rocks. Not really rocks but big seed kind of things. Well, these bastards had ropes on the thing. One pair pulls the head down, the other pulls the middle from the other way. One group lets go, and then the other. The tree comes whipping back up, the honking big seed gets tossed loose. They can hurl that damn seed a long damn way, boss. The seed not only is heavy, but it's got thorns all over it. You don't want to be on the receiving end of this thing."

"Even the damn trees can kill us. This planet is hell," Captain Huzi muttered.

"The trees can kill us with these big fellows pulling on the trees with ropes," Ed snapped, then took two deep breaths and spoke calmly. "Maggie, how many bodies did my *Revenge* leave for you?"

"It's hard to say. There is this fire burning around here, but most of it has burned out. I'd say we found twenty dead big fellows. There's a pretty big trail where the others ran off. Boss, you want me to trail them?"

"You think you can catch them?" Calico asked.

"They're running. We're gunning. I don't see a problem. Besides, if we run into trouble, we can always holler for some of those damn lasers in orbit."

Calico looked around the room. Heads nodded.

"Go after them. Maybe if we kill them all, the others will get it through their thick heads that it's a really bad idea to cause us trouble."

"I'm on it boss. See you tomorrow. Maybe the next day."

Calico looked around the room, his face hot, his eyes burning. "Double the guards on everything. Double the watch tonight. Get that wall up and people on it."

He paused, then turned to Ed. "What about using the lasers in orbit to cut back on the jungle? Get it burning and any of those damn slingshot trees cut in half?"

"That sounds like a good idea," Ed agreed, and made the call.

Five minutes later, the heavens opened up and the fire fell from it. Across the river from the town, the jungle began to burn.

"That ought to teach those bastards," Calico Jack said to Ed Lehrer. He started on his second bottle of rum.

Ed left Calico getting dead drunk. He and Number Two took the next shuttle up. If they were going to slash and burn the jungle, they'd better do it to a plan.

13

———

General Ray Longknife watched as a the 1st Guard Battalion broke into four companies and marched aboard the waiting heavy cruisers. Rita had outdone herself.

The waiting ships weren't just heavy cruisers, they were four of the just completed Astute class. Completed too late for the war, they'd gone directly into mothballs.

Now, Rita had command of four of them and their 9.2-inch lasers.

"God help anything that gets in our way," Ray said, grinning from ear to ear.

"Amen," his wife answered.

"How'd you manage this?"

"I asked for them," she said, simply. "I asked for them and then sent out a call for any of my old pilot officers who weren't knocked up or making milk for their youngster. Despite what you men claimed, most of us girls in uniform did know how to keep our panties on and weren't just dying for the war to end so we could jump in bed with you."

"I'm glad *you* were," Ray said, and covered any leer with a chuckle.

Maybe he didn't do as good a job as he'd thought. She slugged his arm.

But not too hard.

"We kind of needed Alex to end that war, didn't we?"

"And a war was never better ended," Ray agreed.

His wife's eyes got distant. She'd been ready to pay the highest price to end the slaughter. Or let him pay the ultimate price.

Both of them shook their heads at the memory.

"Anyway, by hook or crook, I've knocked together a crew for my ship, the *Astute*. Dan Taussig has the *Artful*. He's a good driver and doesn't mind that half his officers are women. Bessy Milard has the *Alacrity*. She broke into the transports before I did. Paid a high price to be the first. She deserves a warship. Nori Campbell will have the *Arduous*."

Ray frowned. "New ships. New crews. Are they safe in space?"

"I'd prefer to have more time to shake down," Rita admitted, "but I'd rather have them in space than not. We can put it all together on the way there. And once we're at Savannah, maybe we can do more drills to work up while we figure out what those damn pirates are up to. Or not up to."

"Oh, they're up to something," Ray said. "Bad actors like that are always up to something. The only question is what?"

Ray followed Rita aboard the *Astute*. Within three hours, they were under way.

That night, as they settled into bed, Ray risked the big question. "You miss having Alex in the next room?"

"You mean do I miss having Alex nibbling at my breasts? Right now, they feel like they're about to explode."

"That shot to dry you out isn't working as advertised?"

"Whatever does? Anyway, I'm only too glad to have you sharing my room," she said, nuzzling close to him. "And while my teenage self thought my mother was just the worst thing in the world, it's strange how being a mother myself has changed my view of mom."

"She wasn't so bad after all?"

"Not nearly as bad today as she was a couple of years ago. Besides, Alex is so young, how bad can a grandmother do with a one-year old?"

On that, the two of them concentrated on each other. Morning would come all too soon.

Rita was a hard ship driver. She had her small squadron going through every drill in the book, and then invented a few more. Ray didn't have time on his hands, either. He was finding out that being desk bound had not been good for him. Back with the line beasts, he was humping his twenty-kilogram rucksack up ship ladders and down passageways.

It was good to fall into bed exhausted.

Half-way to Savannah, the message traffic began to grab their attention. The pirates were still very much noticeable by their absence. It was the scout ships that were making life challenging.

Two more private ventures had failed to return. More interesting, two of the scout cruisers, the ones that were only supposed to nibble at the unknown, reported back sightings of ball-type ships in systems not all that far from human space.

In both cases, the ships, ours and the puff balls, had flipped ship and headed back the way they'd come. Still, if the aliens were scouting this close to human space, it was not good.

No sooner had they docked than Izzy Umboto of the light cruiser *Patton* and the head of her Marine detachment, one Terry Tordon, Trouble to all, were asking to come aboard.

Trouble was sporting the single star of a brigadier general.

"What happened to you, Marine?" Ray asked as soon as he got a good look at Trouble's uniform.

"A brevet rank. I'm still just the major you got me promoted to after that shindig up on Black Mountain."

"He's commanding the budding Savannah army," Izzy said. "I still make him salute me. I figure a real Navy captain outranks a pretend Marine general any day."

"We try not to see each other until it's too late to salute," Trouble said with a grin.

"What kind of an army does Savannah have?" Rita asked, getting past all the male testosterone vapors.

"We've stood up six regiments of infantry with light support weapons," Trouble explained. "Getting the necessary support elements is a bigger problem. Savannah supplied its old army right off the economy. There was never any intent to deploy it. Getting our own support elements is a bit of a problem. I've offered several commissions in the reserves to some good supply types. They're still talking it over among themselves. It seems some of them have heard bad things about me," Trouble said, buffing his fingernails innocently.

"No doubt all true," Izzy said. "But what brings the two of you to my town? Me, I was just thinking about taking the old *Patton* out for a couple of weeks. Do some scouting myself. I find the rumors coming in of strange ships a bit disturbing."

"If you go," Ray said, "I hope you'll coordinate with us. Wardhaven has a half dozen Rambler class scouts out. They are, no doubt, the source of your rumors."

"I'd be glad to listen to any suggestion you might have," said Izzy, the sailor who'd been a ship captain when most of those listening were still JOs, said.

"Have you heard anything about Whitebred and his pirates?" Rita asked.

Izzy shook her head. "Not a thing. No planets raided. No freighters missing in human space. If I didn't know it couldn't happen, I'd say hell opened up and swallowed every last one of them scoundrels."

"A nice wish, but not likely," Rita said.

"So, you going to drop down and do the party scene?" Izzy asked.

"Not if we can avoid it," Rita and Ray said together.

"Well, I don't see how you can, since I've been empowered by the president to shanghai your souls. He and a dozen business types want to see you about what's happening on the heavy space industry front."

"Is there a problem?" Rita asked.

"As I understand it," Izzy said, "everything is going great. I think they want to tell you all about it. Maybe even thank you, hard as that may be."

"How's the new gear working out at the yards," Rita asked. "Dan Taussig's *Artful* has one reactor that's spent most of the trip out here going up and down like a yo-yo."

"If the work they just did for the *Patton* is any measure, they're going great. I've had the *Patton* tied up to the pier so long, I was afraid to take her out without someone looking under the hood. They did find a few things I wouldn't want to go sick, lame or lazy out there where no gal has gone before."

So the *Artful* was moved to the new Nuu Yards on High Savannah and Ray and Rita shuttled down that evening to talk shop over cocktails with some very committed shipbuilders.

All of them wondered where the pirates had gone. Since the aliens were still not a subject for general conversation, Ray and Rita could only shake their heads in wonder at the pirates' sudden loss of interest in human space.

Rita and Ray found themselves exchanging glances with Izzy and Trouble as they wondered more and more if the smattering of alien ball ships had anything to do with the strange behavior from the pirates.

14

Captain Edmon Lehrer studied the problem of providing support for the troops on the ground and didn't like the looks of what he saw. Even his own *Queen Anne's Revenge* had two more lasers down. They were cannibalizing one to get the other one back up and it looked like a third was coming down with aches and pains.

Fortunately, the chief gunner's mate thought they could strip a subassembly from the cannibalized laser to solve that problem, too.

But how many more problems will I have if I start using those lasers? And what's the status on the other ships?

He called a net conference with Anne Bonney and Grace O'Malley.

"Yeah, I'm down a laser too," Grace admitted. "Any chance I could borrow a cup of sugar from you?" she didn't quite coo.

"If that's what it takes to get lasers up and in business, you can have the damn sugar bowl," Ed said.

"I'll let you know what it is I really need. Who knows, maybe some of what's on my dead lasers can help you out."

"Are we going to have to do this on our own?" Anne asked.

"Do you trust any of those other ships to have a hot laser and know how to shoot straight? We'll need to juggle our places in orbit. I trust we three to provide support to Calico Jack on call. I'm not so sure about the others."

"Forget the 'not sure,' I'll come out and say it," Grace said. "Most of Billy Maynard's crews can't tell one end of a screw driver from the other, and are more likely to use it for a sex toy than a tool. I don't know about Calico Jack's two ships. He's got most of his crew dirtside. Maybe we should lend a few gunners to his ships."

"But we can't cut our crewing too close. We do need to get some serious dirt time to keep our health," Anne pointed out.

"So you see the problem," Ed said. The other two nodded back at him.

An hour later they adjusted orbits and by the end of the day the *Queen Anne's Revenge*, the *Happy Highway Wench* and the *Proper Daughter's Revenge* were spaced at thirty minute intervals around the planet with their orbits regularized enough so that the three of them would be in shooting range of the town and forts for at least twenty minutes of each ninety-minute orbit.

Just how important that was became clear when Ed distributed his shooting plan for burning off the jungle around the settlement.

His, Grace, and Anne's ships met their assigned shoots. Calico's ships met about half of theirs. The rest of the crews were worse. A few didn't even manage to get one shot off.

"It's bad," Ed said when the three again met on net.

"We're pirates, Ed, not Navy ships," Anne pointed out.

"We're pirates that have bit off one huge mouthful of

snakes," Grace said. "Ed, are you thinking about pulling up your coattails and running?"

"Not yet, I'm not. But I certainly am keeping it front and center in my mind," Ed admitted. "If I have to run, I'd sure like to have some more gold in my chest."

"And I damn well don't want to run when all we got to worry about is some simpletons that are throwing nasty seed pods at us," Anne said, with vehemence.

"No, I'm not going to run away from some super coconuts," Ed agreed.

Two days later, after burning a lot of jungle from orbit, Ed found out what he might just want to run away from.

15

Black Bart was hollering as soon as *Your Bad Day* was in the system. "I found out where they're taking the gold, and boy was it easy picking getting it back."

Ben Hornigold was just as excited . . . and uninformative . . . when his ship, now named *The Golden Mist*, jumped through.

As soon as Bart made orbit, all the captains shuttled down to meet at the Captain's house. It was the old governor's house with the new name over the door. Ed caught Annie and Grace's eyes, and together they settled in at the end of the table close to the door. With them there, the other skippers who had followed Ed from LeMonte took their places around them as if it was the head of the table.

That left Billy Maynard at the other end of the table with Black Bart at his right and Ben Hornigold at his left. The rest of the captains from Port Elgin took over the other end of the table and seemed to think they were at the head.

Calico Jack arrived late from an expedition he'd been leading into the jungle. He smelled like it too, but pulled up a chair at Ed's right, between him and Grace.

Despite the stink, she flashed Jack an encouraging smile, not that he needed one.

Black Bart called for drinks all around, then stood as bottles were passed out. "This drink is on me. I've found the pot of gold at the end of the rainbow."

Bottles clinked, heartily at one end of the table, more cautiously at Ed's end.

"So, how'd you find this end of the rainbow?" Billy Maynard asked.

"I spotted this ball ship just before it ducked through a jump," Bart said.

"*We* spotted this ball ship," Ben cut in.

"Yeah, I guess we did. Anyway, we followed it real care-ful-like. If we did a jump and it was still in the system, we would duck back fast."

"Though we'd stay long enough to figure out which jump it was goin' to," Ben added.

"So, we did this for four . . ."

"No. Five jumps," Ben insisted.

"And there was that ship, headed for this lovely little planet when we jumped through the fifth jump."

"We headed down there," Ben said, taking over the story, to Bart's clear disapproval. "When that puff ball caught sight of us, it forgot the planet and took off running. Real cool-like, we sauntered up to that planet, and damned if there weren't several towns."

"We picked the biggest burg," Bart said, taking back over the story. "There were these same big dudes. Some had guns this time, so there was a bit of a fight."

"The big fellows back here had guns," Calico Jack put in. "Some of us remember fighting them."

"Well, we did remember you lazing them from space,"

Ben said. "'Cause that was what we did to them. We fried them good."

"All but the center of town," Bart said. "We left it pretty much alone, and it was a good thing we did, 'cause that was where they had all the gold and jewels. God, did they have a shit load of that nice stuff. I think they really like it. Maybe as much as us. So, we loaded up the *Bad Day* and the *Golden Mist* and here we are, rich as God. You ought to head over there and collect up some of what we left behind."

There was a lot of cheering, and clinking of jugs, at least at that end of the table. Ed folded his hands across his chest and just stared at Billy.

It took a while, but Billy Maynard finally seemed to feel Ed's gaze and looked down the table at where he and his captains sat.

Billy rapped the table with his empty rum jug and got silence. "Ed, you don't look all that happy. You got a problem with this?"

"Kind of. Yes, Billy. As Ben and Bart tell this, they followed a big fellow's ship back to that planet."

"Yep," Bart said.

"So what's to say that they didn't follow you two back here?"

The room got real quiet.

"It don't matter if they did. Them big fellows got no fight in them," Black Bart said.

"Did anyone follow you?" Ed demanded. He didn't miss the fact that Bart hadn't said a word about being followed.

"We did see a ship," Ben admitted, "but it didn't follow us."

"How often did you see the ship?" Grace O'Malley demanded. "Twice? Three times?"

"Two, maybe three," Bart admitted.

"Oh, shit," Calico Jack said.

"But what's it matter?" Billy said. "They got no balls for a fight. Just look at what we've got here."

"These people are miners. Mere peasants," said Kim. He spoke as a captain for the farmers back home and pike men here. "You killed their soldiers and have conquered peasants, men of the earth that have no more interest in fighting your wars than I do. Maybe less. But when you talked of gold, me and mine chose to fight. Are you sure these peasants of the earth are not waiting for their soldier class to come back and stomp you into the mud?"

That started an uproar in the room.

Some looked ready to take Kim out and lynch him. The thin man moved over to stand behind Ed's chair. Ed and Calico Jack pulled pistols from their holsters and laid them flat on the table.

And kept their hands close to them.

When the room quieted down to a dull roar, Calico Jack said, "The man has a point," in that quiet, deadly voice he had.

The room got a lot quieter.

Then Jack's commlink buzzed. Without taking his eyes from the other end of the table, he tapped it. "Yes."

"Boss, all hell's breaking loose," came in a half-hysterical shriek that Ed recognized as Maggie's.

"What kind of hell?" Jack demanded.

"These bastards, they got us in an ambush. We got several guys that tumbled into pit traps when they tried to take cover. Now these big fellows got explosives and they can really throw them. Boy can they pitch 'em."

That was punctuated on net by an explosion, quickly followed by two more.

"They got those damn bending trees, only they're using them to shoot sticks at us,"

"Arrows," Kim provided beside Calico Jack.

"Yeah, it's like bows and arrows," Maggie agreed. "We're shooting but we ain't got no targets to shoot at."

A glance out the window showed full dark.

There were more explosions on net. "We're running. Oh!"

There was a shriek and other noises from the commlink. "Oh, shit," Maggie said matter-of-factly. "I fell in one of their damn pits. Right on a big sharp stick." What started as a groan shot up into a shriek. "Shit, it hurts, Jack! Help me!"

Then the commlink went dead.

"Jack, I've got a report on explosions about ten klicks out of town," Ed said, passing along what his Number Two who was manning the wall had just told him on net.

"That's where I left them when I got called back here," Calico Jack said, already heading for the door.

Then he froze. There were shots coming from outside the Captain's House.

16

Captain Edmon Lehrer grabbed for his pistols on the table. With one in each hand, and Anne and Grace as well armed at each elbow, he followed Calico Jack.

He paused at the door to look out. There was a flash somewhere, then the sound of an explosion loud and soon.

"That wasn't ten klicks out," Grace said.

"No," Calico agreed, then he shoved open the door and dashed for a pile of boxes a couple of meters away.

Ed came up to the door. He looked both ways. In the dark, figures were moving. Some bigger, some smaller. Rifle muzzles flashed . . . and not all of them were from the smaller figures. Ed dashed for a spot beside Calico.

An explosion flashed not a hundred meters down the street. The screams were human, but in the flash of light, Ed could make out big fellows. Lots of them.

He fired and one spun backwards.

But another one picked up the pike that one dropped and drove it into a fleeing human.

Calico shot and the big one fell, but another was picking up the pike before it hit the ground. Another had scooped up a rifle dropped by the human.

That big one ducked behind a barrel before Ed could put a shot in him.

A moment later, shots drove Ed to duck.

"Quick learners," Calico said.

"Smarter than some of the fools in that meeting we were wasting time in," Ed spat.

A ceramic jar with a sputtering fuse dropped behind them and rolled away. Grace O'Malley didn't miss a step, but changed her leap to join them to one of scooping up the jar and hurling it back.

This time it hit something, burst and then began to burn with a struggling light.

Ed fired at a shape that moved in that light. The scream that was his reward came from no human throat.

"Cover me," Calico said, and made ready to race up the street toward a water trough. Grace and Ed put both of their pistols up and fired as rapidly as they could pull the triggers while Calico low-ran up the street.

By the time he was back under cover, Anne had joined them.

"Shoot while we reload," Ed said, and she kept up the fire while he popped out the magazines from his two pistols and slammed a new one in each. He slipped the empties into his shirt pocket. If this kept up, he'd have to find time to reload them.

"And find cartridges," he muttered to himself.

"Don't tell me, Ed, that you didn't bring a small armory to this shindig," Grace said.

"Three mags each, then I got to find some ammo."

"Check my bag, boy. There's a hundred-round box under my tampons. And don't mess with those, it's a bad month."

"I won't," Ed said, and turned at something he'd caught out of the corner of his eye. A big fellow was charging at them with a lowered pike.

He put four rounds between that one's eyes, an easy enough thing, with all those eyes to shoot for, and the big one skidded into the dust, the pike stopping just inches from Anne's foot.

"Thanks," Anne said.

"Think nothing of it."

Further up the street, Calico had slipped into a barracks and returned to the street with an automatic rifle with a grenade launcher under the barrel. He had two bandoleers, one of grenades the other of rifle ammo slung over his shoulders.

He emptied the rifle at full rock and roll at the shadows in the next alley. There were screams and a fused jug rolled out to explode harmlessly in the middle of the street.

"What are you doing back there?" Calico shouted, reloading. "Get up here and empty this armory before those bastards get at it."

"You heard the man," Grace said, and with Calico covering for them, she made a dash to the barracks, drew a carbine with rocket launcher, grabbed a bandolier of ammo for each of them, and rejoined Calico.

Ed took a few moments to wave a couple of his captains from the door where they'd been bunching up. "You cover down the street that way," he ordered, and two of them ran for a couple of rain barrels while another two pirates provided cover.

Where the hell are Billy and his bad boys? Ed thought, but

Calico was waving for him to make a run for the barracks and its armory. He waved for one more of his captains to make a run for the guns, then followed him.

It was nice to trade his pistols in for a big magazine rifle and grenade launcher. He sent the last captain back to provide cover for the crew he'd sent down the street and joined Jack and the gals looking up the street.

"You take that side of the street," Calico Jack said, motioning Ed to the right. "I'll take this side. Gals, pick your man and back us up."

"Back you up, hell," Grace snapped, and leaped out ahead of them. Anne was running for the far side, so Ed followed her, firing at anything that moved. Too many of the figures sprawled down in the street looked small and limited in legs and arms.

It was a bad night and likely to get worse.

From the looks of it, the bastards had gotten loose and started the killing before any human sounded the alarm.

They worked their way up the street, shooting at anything that moved. They shot a lot of empty shadows, but they got themselves a few big fellows, too.

At the end of the street were the pens where the big fellows were supposed to spend their nights.

They were empty.

"No surprise here," Calico muttered.

"How'd they get loose?" Grace asked.

"Your guess is as good as mine," Calico said, "but I doubt that ambush out in the jungle and this break out are accidents in timing. They've been working on this."

"Wouldn't you if you got a look at what we did at Fort Four," Anne said.

"They weren't supposed to see it," Ed said.

"They got four eyes," Grace said. "How blind do you expect them to be?

Ed looked around for the big fellows. He didn't have to look a lot.

"The wall," Calico Jack hollered. "They're trying to make it over the wall."

Sure enough, at the end of the road, there was a break in the wall for the road out. A half-dozen big bastards, two with guns, the others with pikes, were storming the gate guards.

Anne opened fire, but missed. The big ones spotted the fire from behind and the two with rifles turned to take them under fire while the other four kept up the charge with lowered pikes. Even as Ed fired, one of them took a pirate at the gate full in the neck.

The body went one way, the head the other and suddenly there was another four-eyed bastard to pick up the pike and swing it at a kid that was cringing in the shadow of the gate. He skewered the youngster and raised his body high, blood splattering.

Ed knew he needed to duck from the incoming rifle fire, but he knew the kid. He was from Ed's crew. The youth who had started the trouble up at Fort Four.

Ed blew away the big one, even as a slug took him in the arm.

He dropped down behind some crates, cussing his bad luck and stupidity.

"It bad?" Anne asked.

"It hurts like hell, but I can move my fingers and nothing's broke."

Anne tore a strip of cloth from the bottom of her shirt and wrapped it around the bleeding cut. "Nothing's spurting. You got more luck than you deserve," she said.

"Thanks for caring."

"Don't we all," she said, and gave him a quick kiss for no good reason before grabbing her rifle and returning fire.

Ed found himself grimacing at the pain and trying to work up enough nerve to stick his head back up and shoot some bastard with too many eyes.

As it turned out, it was good that he was looking the wrong way.

He spotted movement down by the river. The wall there wasn't as tall, what with the river being a good two hundred meters across there. Tall or not, Ed spotted big forms with too many arms and legs rolling over the wall.

He pulled up his rifle and took a shot. Maybe he hit something. Maybe the big bastard just rolled over the wall. It was hard to tell in the dark.

"They're going into the river," Ed shouted.

Calico Jack turned, eyed the river wall for a moment as a half-dozen big ones rolled over it, then took them under fire.

"The attack on the gate was a diversion," he shouted. "They're headed into the river. Ed, you and Annie try to keep the gate in our hands. Grace, with me."

"You bet," Grace shouted, and the two of them headed for the river.

"Cover them!" Annie shouted, and Ed did his best. He was up and shooting, putting his now vulnerable flesh at risk. He got one of the shooters, but another soon picked it up.

So Ed shot that one.

And something sailed over the wall with a fuse sputtering against the night. It exploded before it hit, sending shards of pottery flying, but none close to Ed and Annie.

More followed. Some exploded early. Others hit first. They either caught fire or did nothing.

Annie and Ed kept up their fire, cutting down more shooters but other big bastards stepped in to take their place. Still, it couldn't last. There was only so much ammunition. The guns fell silent. From further down the wall, humans advanced, shooting.

The big fellows with the pikes formed a rough line and charged Ed and Annie.

They shot them down to a man. Or bastard. It was hard knowing what words to use.

Ed and Annie ran for the gate . . . and got there just as a rough line of big fellows with bows and clubs were coming out of the jungle, two hundred meters out.

They cut them down with rapid fire and the smart ones that survived fell back.

To his right, Ed could hear Calico Jack and Grace making their own way toward the river wall. There was a lot of rapid fire punctuated by a few single rifle shots. Those were usually answered by a grenade explosion.

Ed kicked himself. He'd forgotten, in the heat of battle, that he did have a grenade launcher and grenades.

"I guess that's why we train grunts," he muttered to himself . . . and loaded a grenade, held his rifle at a forty-five-degree angle and sent a round arching out into the jungle.

The big bastards answered him with a couple of their own fused shells, and something else. These rounds came in big sacks with a couple of fuses.

Where they hit, fire exploded. Tents began to burn. The few remaining thatched huts caught fire with an eagerness that was stunning to watch.

"What's in those sacks?" Ed asked.

"I don't know," Annie said, "but it stinks to high heaven."

Their contemplation of what was happening behind

them had to be postponed as shapes began to form up in the thinned jungle ahead of them. They took turns lobbing grenades at the near threat while sending some out as far as they could in the hopes of catching whoever it was burning the place down.

Around midnight, things finally got quiet.

17

Captain Edmon Lehrer rubbed his eyes as dawn lit the eastern sky. If his looked like Annie's, they were red as a cut throat. The smoke and the stink from the fire bombs irritated the hell out of his eyes, his nose, this throat, his lungs. He hacked up crap from his sore throat and spit it out.

"Do you think there's anything poisonous in that fire shit they tossed at us?" Annie asked.

Ed shrugged. "We're alive and still hurting, ain't we?"

They half chuckled at his half joke.

Ed and Captain Annie Bonney now stood on the wall beside the opening they called the South Gate. It would be nice if they actually had a gate to close, but for now, it was just a gaping hole where there was no wall and no moat in front of it.

Some of the younger farm kids had put aside their pole weapons and lugged sand bags up here, so now Ed was able to hunker down with his borrowed rifle and look everything over without worrying about being picked off by one of the rifles the big bastards had taken.

Or one of their long arrows.

The kids who lugged up the sandbags had taken away the bodies of the earlier defenders of the wall that hadn't managed to dodge the arrows or be missed by the bullets.

A shot came from somewhere on the edge of the jungle. The bullet went wide of them. Annie sent a rocket grenade arching out to explode just inside the unburned trees.

"You think you got anything?" Ed asked.

"Your guess is as good as mine," Annie said, wiping her eyes. "But we got to keep them back."

"I wonder what our supply of grenades looks like?" Ed said.

Both of them grimaced.

"At least they ain't good shots," a farm kid said as he added a sandbag to the wall's growing parapet.

"No, they aren't," Annie said. "I don't think our kind of rifles fit all that well in their hands."

"You want to bet me that *their* kind of rifles will fit just fine in the hands of *their* soldiers?" Ed said.

He and Annie shared a scowl at that thought. The kid who'd made the comment slunk away.

Calico Jack joined them. He gave them a tired wave, rested his rifle on the sand bags, muzzle out, and eyed the jungle silently.

"How'd it go on the river side?" Ed asked.

"They swim like fish," Calico said, his voice rough with exhaustion and whatever it was in the air. "They rolled over the wall, scrambled out into the water and dove. I think they can hold their breath for a couple of minutes. Or maybe those things at their throat. Someone thinks they may really be gills."

"I've never seen them use them," Ed said.

"You've never seen them underwater, have you?"

Ed admitted he hadn't.

"Billy wants to have a meeting of the captains right after they have breakfast."

"That's mighty kind of him to be thinking about our stomachs," Annie said. "Where was he when we were fighting for our lives? And his?"

"He says he and his captains were holding the North Gate," Calico said. "Who knows, maybe they were."

Ed turned from the jungle to let his eyes rove over the destruction inside. "Is it as bad as it looks? The town?"

Calico turned to follow his gaze.

"It ain't nice, I can tell you. I don't know what all was in those fire bombs they tossed at us. Animal fat? Some kind of thing like a pine cone that burned like Willie Pete. It didn't matter. We didn't have any water to fight the fires with. You take a bucket to the river and you were as like to be shot with an arrow from the other bank as to be knifed by some big fellow coming at you out of the water."

"Are we besieged?" Annie asked.

"If we aren't, it's close enough not to make any difference to me."

The next couple of kids with sandbags included a young girl with a bucket of water and a sack of bread and cheese. They drank first, then used what was left to wash some of the night's grime from their skin.

The young girl had brought an actual medical kit with her. Annie peeled the blood-soaked bandage off Ed's arm, washed it down with wine, then took a needle to the long slash the bullet had made of his forearm.

Calico pulled off his thick leather belt and gave it to Ed to chew on.

Ed managed not to embarrass himself in front of his

shipmates by screaming. He did put some serious teeth marks in Jack's belt.

About eight, a couple of shipmates from his and Annie's *Revenges* showed up. They got the rifles only after they showed they knew how to use them. That done, the three captains headed for the Captains' House.

"Where's Grace?" Annie asked.

"She took an arrow last night," Calico said, tersely. "I'm hoping to find her at the fort or the house before the meeting.

They increased their pace.

The fort was no longer a treasure house. In the morning light, it was a charnel house.

Dead bodies lined the dusty road in front of it. Inside, living bodies lay on pallets on the floor. Shipmates offered some solace, but medical help was in short supply. Not that many doctors had chosen to flee Savannah; there had been few among the icicles.

Grace, being a captain, was getting the best they had. They found her in an off room, seated at a table with several empty rum bottles strewn before her and a near empty one at her lips.

Her right shoulder was bandaged, but red was seeping through the white.

"How are you?" Annie asked, taking a chair beside her friend.

"Fine. Fine," she slurred. "Better if you can get me a new bottle. Make that three."

Calico turned to go hunt up some more rum.

"No, really, how are you?"

Grace scowled down at her shoulder. "Doc don't think it will ever work quite right, ever again. Ever," she muttered darkly, then seemed to brighten. "You can call me Lefty."

"I'll call you Grace O'Malley, the best pirate skipper in the fleet," Ed said.

"You think the guys will follow a broad with no right wing?"

"You got your arm," Annie said. "With some physical therapy, we'll work you back to as good as new."

"You ever seen a pirate thysical ferapist?" Grace spat,

"I'll find one just for you," Ed said. "Even if I have to go to old Earth to steal him."

"You'd do that for me?" Grace said.

"For you, we'd do anything," Annie said. "Hell, you've had Calico doing just about anything you wanted."

"I did tell you that, didn't I?" Grace said.

"He's hunting you up some more rum," Ed pointed out.

"I've got some more rum," Calico said.

But he'd arrived too late. The rum had finally done its job. Grace O'Malley had just done a face plant on the table.

There was a bed handy. The three of them managed to get Grace from the chair to the bed. Annie removed her boots and they left her snoring softly, her face free of care and pain.

Ed turned to Calico and Annie. "This better be a good meeting."

18

C aptain Edmon Lehrer noted how the captain's table now automatically divided itself in two, just like it had last night. He sat at one end with his captains. Captain Billy Maynard was at the other end with his.

There was no middle.

Kim, along with two of his own farmers, now pike men, had pulled up chairs to sit behind Ed.

Ed wasn't too sure how he felt about being the patron of the farmers, but he liked eating, and it was a farmer's doctor that had patched up Grace.

I guess I owe you a few, Kim, Ed concluded.

"This is a mess you made of things," Captain Huzi said. If he'd been aiming his words at Billy, Ed would have said a hearty amen.

But Huzi was staring hard at Calico Jack.

"What do you mean by that?" Calico shot back.

"You was in charge of the ground sloggin'. You could have kilt all them bastards the first time we seen them all."

"I do remember someone not being all that eager to wade into the river to pan for gold," Annie said dryly.

"But now we gots ourselves a mess 'cause you was soft-hearted," Black Bart said.

"Billy, we going to spend this morning crying over spilt milk?" Ed asked. "It seems to me that what's done is done. What I'm seriously concerned about is what we do next."

"We mow them all down," Huzi shouted.

The room, at least his half, rumbled in agreement.

"How you going to mow what you can't see?" Annie asked.

The room got a bit quieter.

"You're so smart," Billy said. "What do you think we ought to do?"

Since he was locking eyes with Ed when he slammed down that gauntlet, Ed leaned back in his chair and waited for quiet. With the two acknowledged leaders locking silent horns, the room slowly came to silence too.

Into the quiet, Ed took a deep breath. "As I see it, we have a choice to make. Depending on which of two options we pick, we'll have other things to decide, but first we got to get the big one out in the open."

"And that would be?" Billy Maynard said, sassy as ever.

"Do we go or do we stay?" Ed said, tossing the words flat on the table between them.

Again, the room got real noisy. Most of the racket came from the other end of the table. What with Ed, Calico, and Annie sitting with arms folded on their chests and their mouths closed, the talk at his end of the table was limited to a few comments of agreement.

"We can't go," Huzi shouted. And shouted, and shouted enough to quiet that end of the table. He punctuated the quiet with a final, "We can't go!"

He pointed in the general direction of the river. "There's gold out there. And silver. And jewels if we can find them. I ain't walkin' away with my tail between my legs while it's still there for the taking."

Ed eyed Billy. "Is that where you stand?"

Billy didn't seem all that sure of where he stood, but with his captains all kind of agreeing with Huzi, it was pretty clear that if he didn't agree with them, they'd vote him out and put someone else at that end of the table to talk for the rest of them.

"Ain't it nice being a pirate king?" Calico Jack whispered softly.

Annie snickered.

"It seems we're all for staying," Billy said, then rubbed his week-old beard. "But how do we get the gold out of the river and into our pockets?"

The question got some comments rolling around the table, much like waves upon the sand. And like waves that roar at the beach and then dribble away back to the ocean, the rumblings gave little suggestion of how they should solve their troubles.

"And what do we do with those four eyed bastards while we're getting at our gold?" one captain asked.

"We kill 'em. The only good four-eyed bastard is a dead one," Black Bart offered.

"Do you agree?" Billy asked Ed's end of the table.

Ed tossed that one to Calico Jack with a quick nod.

"Yeah, we're gonna have to kill them," Calico agreed. "We sure can't trust them to pan for gold now, can we?"

The room rumbled agreement.

"But who will pan for *our* gold?" Kim asked from his seat behind Ed.

Ed turned around. "You want to join us at the table?" he asked Kim.

"Don't mind if I do. Assuming you are indeed inviting me."

"As I see it, that gold is even less likely to jump out of the river and into our pockets than any fish swimming around," Ed said. "Anyone see another way?"

The room's assent was there, if softly grumbled.

"We who dig the gold will take a third of it," Kim said, flatly. "How you divide up the other two-thirds will be your own decision."

"A third for you little runts," Huzi exploded, but his was only the first shout. The other end of the table was quickly up in arms. Ed noted that even a few of his captains seemed unhappy with the demand, but they kept their mouths shut, leaving it to him to show he knew best how to protect their interests.

Ed let the foot stomping and shouting die down quite a bit before he said softly, "If they don't do the panning, there won't be a gram for the rest of us. Of course, if you want, you can do the panning and let them have the rifles and stand watch on the beach for the big bastards."

The room got quiet again.

"As I see it," Calico Jack began, "We're going to need a lot of cooperation here, or we might as well put our tails between Captain Huzi's legs and slink away. Now that the big bastards have got all their people out of our hands, I don't know what they'll do. Maybe they'll retreat into the jungle, wait, like Kim mentioned a bit ago, for their Navy and Soldiers to come up and slap us down."

The room got real quiet as some very thick heads contemplated that prospect.

"It's fine with me if they do that," Calico Jack said. "I'd

grab for all I could get my hands on, keep a good weather eye out for them balls entering the system, and then run like hell with the loot. We've done that plenty of times before."

Some heads were nodding along with Calico.

Not Hornigold and Black Bart. "I say we shot them down. This is our planet. I ain't for giving it back to nobody."

"We can make that call when we see how many balls come through the jump," Ed said, dodging the question for the moment. He hoped the way he said it made it clear that he'd be very cautious when he made that call.

His skippers nodded along with him.

"I'm for fighting. Period. My momma didn't have no yellow kids," Black Bart grumbled.

"Okay," Calico Jack said, "we seem to be arriving at a policy. We'll pan for gold. Maybe get the silver mine working again. We'll guard the gold panners and the mine. We'll use what we got in orbit to brush back any big collection of them we spot anywhere in the jungle. We might even send a few expeditions into the jungle to make sure they keep their distance."

"Not under your command," Huzi snapped.

"I'd go for a walk in the jungle with Calico," Annie said.

"In the moonlight," came from somewhere at the other end of the table.

"I think we'll keep our punitive expeditions to daylight for now," Jack said.

"So, we seem to have an agreement," Captain Billy Maynard said. "Any of them big bastards we see, we shoot on sight. With anything we got up to and including 6-inch lasers."

The room roared its agreement.

"Our little friends here will pan for gold. Maybe do some digging for silver, too."

The room eyed Kim. He gave a shallow bow from the waist. "For one third of all gold we retrieve. The same for the silver."

"Of course," Billy said, and his pledge was as good as any ever made to a girl after midnight.

"We'll decide how to split up the rest," Billy said.

"Why don't we do it now?" Ed suggested. "Half of it for guards here on the ground. The other half for those in orbit."

"Why should someone cool and comfortable up there get as much as I get for sweating down here," came from one of Billy's skippers.

"Because our 6-inch lasers may save your ass when you need it saved," Annie shot right back. "Assuming some ships can get their lasers working." She was looking hard at Black Bart when she said that.

"I can fire when I have to." he snarled back.

"And hit what you're aiming at?" Annie said.

"Sashay your ass over here and I'll show you what I can hit," the pirate leered, and balled up his fist.

Suddenly Annie's pistol was in her hand, her aim right between Black Bart's eyes.

"Or not," the pirate said, now eyes only for the table.

"Ed, keep your hellion under control," Billy said. "We don't draw no guns at the Captains' Table."

"Annie," Ed said.

Her pistol went back into its holster.

"I think we have an agreement," Ed said. "I'm assuming that Calico Jack will continue as our ground captain."

"He ain't done so good," Huzi muttered, but no one offered up a different name for a ground captain, and none of them were stupid enough to suggest that the pirates didn't need someone in charge of setting up their dirtside defenses.

Not after last night.

"Calico Jack will lead the ground defenses," Billy agreed. "I expect him to give us some idea of what he's intended on doing before he does it."

"I think that can be arranged."

"May I ask one question?" Annie said, before the meeting could break up.

"And what might it be?" Billy said.

"What's our food and ammunition situation?"

Ed and Billy found themselves eyeing each other. Ed was the first to raise a quizzical eyebrow. "Maybe we should send back to Port Elgin and LeMonte for some food."

"And send someone with some gold to buy up some ammo," Annie added with a dimpled smile, "Don't you just hate it when a gal is right?"

19

cting Captain Constantine Odinkalu was having a very nice time of it. When Captain Edmon Lehrer tapped him to take over the LeMonte colony while the gold-fevered types ran off to seek their fortune, he was none too sure he could handle matters.

If it hadn't been for some poor investments to people of rather shady means, he would much rather have preferred to stay and try his hand at the new Savannah. Then, of course, there were the three women who didn't remember saying yes. Or maybe he had misheard them.

Anyway, he'd ended up on Whitebred, or LeMonte as it was now, not at all fitting in with the other inmates of this asylum.

Then again, most of the people he didn't fit in with had rushed aboard ship and taken off for points unknown, or at least not all that well known. Even the more adventurous icicles had grabbed anything sharp and followed the gold lust.

That left the meek, or at least more careful, as they liked

to tell themselves, planting crops and becoming rather more like a normal colony with every passing day.

Conny had even agreed to thaw out more farmers, now that they had enough food to feed more people. The scenes of men collecting their wives. Of boyfriends rejoining their girlfriends, with trips to the altar soon after, was heart-warming.

Hopefully, Captain Lehrer wouldn't mind too much. The local governor who'd replaced Kim, however, had been most persuasive. "Happy farmers work harder, my friend. Give us our wives."

He'd given them their wives, and even turned loose some of the women who'd been unfrozen and used by the pirates. There had been some harsh words about that, but as Conny had told them, "You're getting them back. There's nothing more I can do."

On the whole, he had a happy colony.

Then it got complicated.

Grace O'Malley showed up, her arm in a sling, demanding a couple of tons of wheat, rice, and corn.

"I don't have that much," Conny told her.

"But the last harvest was supposed to be good."

"Yes," Conny agreed, "but I woke a lot of the sleepers. The farmers wanted their wives and sweethearts."

"Shit, Conny, Ed's going to skin you alive when he hears this."

Conny blanched. Captain Edmon Lehrer was a decent kind of man. For a pirate. What he'd do when pressed . . .?

"Did you find gold?" Conny said, trying to change the subject.

"More than you ever dreamed of," she said, and smiled. It was a nice smile, though it had a lot of teeth showing.

"Well, maybe you could use some of the gold to buy food," Conny said, tentatively.

"We didn't *steal* the gold to *spend* it on food," Grace said. Then seemed to lose herself in thought. "You know anywhere we could get ammo? Lots of ammo and grenades?"

"I don't know anyplace much, except Savannah."

Grace eyed him. "But you knew your way around Savannah pretty well, didn't you?"

Conny didn't like the look on her face. "Kind of," he said, and swallowed hard.

"Son, you need to get one of those dock queens away from the pier. You and me, we're going grocery shopping. For ammo and grenades, and if you're a good boy, I'll even buy a couple of hundred tons of food that, if the price is right, might mean that Ed will let you keep your skin."

Captain Rita Nuu-Longknife was happy, but bored. No, make that Commodore Nuu-Longknife. She commanded a squadron of big heavy cruisers and had been granted the honor of being called commodore.

The pay was the same, but she was supposed to be impressed with the honor.

Honor didn't matter a hill of beans to her. If she'd known they'd be sitting so long on their rumps above Savannah, she'd have brought little Alex along and set up house-keeping in the station hotel.

As it was, she missed Alex, and she and Ray were hardly keeping house out of her in-port cabin. They weren't there all that much.

Yes, she could coordinate the scouting fleet from her ship tied alongside the station. It was Ray who was spending most of his days out of sight. He'd shuttled his battalion of Wardhaven Guard down to the planet and was exercising them with Trouble's raw recruits from Savannah.

If she had it right, Trouble had been a captain in the

Society Marines that beat Ray off that little moon and damn near got him and her killed.

It was hard to see men who'd been busy trying to kill each other just a year or so ago hoisting beers and talking about old times as if they'd been best of friends since forever.

Then again, Rita had hired Andy Anderson, the skipper of the defense brigade that Trouble had belonged to. And she was regularly talking over ship handling with Captain Izzy Umbota who had been in the Society of Humanity Navy long before Rita managed to talk and finagle her way aboard an attack transport.

And Rita was learning that commanding a transport was one long mile away from skippering a big heavy cruiser. These damn things had systems on them that broke every time you looked at them crooked. She'd wondered why the Navy spent so much time tied up at the pier. Now she knew. Just getting her four cruisers out here to Savannah had racked up a fix and mend list an arm long.

And the new yard. Or correctly, the Nuu Yard's gear was still teething. It seemed that they were working the kinks out of their gear on *her* ships.

She did not think much of that honor, and she told her dad so.

His message back started with him laughing at her, had some good advice in the middle, and ended with him laughing.

So, Rita spent more time having her officers and sailors run more tests, drills and, in general, figuring out what needed fixing without running up the cost of an underway day.

It was hard to believe how much it cost just to meet a payday for the ship's crew. If you dared to take one away from the pier for a day, it cost an arm and a leg. Then the other arm and leg to fix what broke when it was out in space.

Why the hell were war ships so damn fragile?

"Money," Rita growled in exasperation, then remembered. Thanks to her luck at birth, dad had seen to it that she never lacked for anything. Now, what she needed was the obscene amount that it cost to run a fleet, and she was acting like a kid who wanted a pony for Christmas and was threatening to throw a tantrum because she only got a four-wheel drive toy.

But that wasn't all that was bugging her. She'd pulled on just about every string she knew about to get a scouting fleet out to find those damn pirates.

Everything!

She had a whole lot of ships out in space hunting for the pirates.

So what was she finding?

Nothing! Not a damn thing!

How did that old song go about the king who marched up the hill and then marched back down again? Was it a king or maybe some other title? Who could keep straight all the different things they called people back before they all had to work for a living.

Anyway, she had marched a whole lot of ships out to the rim, up the hill, so to speak, and what had she found? Nothing.

It was going to be very hard to march them back again.

But she'd have to do it pretty soon. Money was running out and without any new ships going missing, the insurance rates were settling back down to their usual level. No one wanted to waste money looking for pirates that weren't there.

Exasperated, Rita scrawled her signature on another requisition chit. She hoped they'd have enough money to cover the cost of rewiring the damn superconducting magnetohydrodynamic track on the *Artful*. The ship shouldn't have needed that replaced so soon. No doubt, it was a bad bit of work from her father's yard.

She thought for a moment about demanding the work for free, but, no doubt, whatever guarantee had been given to the Unity government wasn't worth the paper it was printed on now. And the Unity thugs had taken their bribes for shoddy work and run, or been hanged, or something worse.

No, the ships were hers now, and she'd just have to figure out a way to keep them running.

Until time ran out on all of them.

She smiled. The new Astute class was being called the Arguable class within her hearing, and the Asshole class when she wasn't supposed to hear. Sailors.

"Honey, you home?" came in Ray's delightful voice.

"Were else would I be? I don't dare take the ships out for fear something will break and I'll have to dredge up money to pay the repair bill."

"Everything costs money," Ray said, coming to give her a 'time to quit work' kiss.

She kissed him back harder.

"That tasted like a 'stay home tonight' kiss," he said.

"Can we?"

He shook his head. "There's another reception downside tonight at the old Society Embassy. I forget what they're calling it now, but I need to be there. Next week, we want to take Trouble's kids out to the rifle range and let them shoot their rifles. Strange that soldiers should actually get to shoot at something."

"It's even stranger when sailors get to shoot," Rita said, dryly.

"Anyway, there's a shortage of small arms ammunition and what there is available has doubled in price."

"Strange that," Rita said, puzzled. "Is there a war on and nobody told me?"

"Trust me, I'd be the first to hear," Ray said. "Anyway, the presidents of the two companies that make the small arms ammunition will be at the reception and it's my one chance to get them in a corner and bend their elbows about meeting the contracts they signed at the price they agreed to."

Rita frowned. "They signed contracts to provide so much ammo at such and such a price?"

"Yep."

"Dad would be very put out with any subcontractor who reneged on a signed contract. Aren't they just selling you the stuff they already had in stock? Ammo that they maybe took back from those divisions you broke when you were here last?"

"I don't think so," Ray said, but now he was looking puzzled.

"Let's get dressed. I'll help you break a few arms. I'm in the mood to break heads, but, no doubt, the milk of human kindness that flows in your veins will force me to settle for just arms."

"Love of my life, I haven't blown any shit up for two, no, three weeks. I'm about due to let loose a little havoc myself."

21

Major General Ray Longknife looked around the reception at the Society Embassy, on Savannah and found little had changed. It was a bit more dilapidated. The walls were in greater need of a new coat of paint, the carpet a bit more threadbare. The fake flowers were looking down right droopy.

But no one came here for the decor. They came for the conversation or not at all.

He was in his dress dinner uniform. Rita had made a face and pulled one of her civilian gowns from their wardrobe. "I swear, the men who make woman's uniforms hate us," she said, for at least the fiftieth time since they'd met.

Before they'd married, she would have swallowed the issue and worn her uniform; she was so proud to be serving in uniform. Now, she muttered and wore something that left Ray wishing his dinner dress still included a sword he could use to cut it off her.

He could also use it to fight off the civilians who would

be enjoying the way Rita's no longer otherwise employed, but not yet shrunken down to size, breasts filled that gown.

He spotted Becky Graven, the Foreign Service Officer who had been his right hand during the recent unpleasantness on Savannah. Or maybe he'd been her right hand.

It was often hard to tell which way it went when good diplomats worked with good troopers.

"I'm glad to see that you two could make it," Becky said to the both of them.

"I wouldn't miss it for the world," Rita lied.

Or did she mean it? Mean that she wasn't about to let Ray loose around Becky.

It's nice when the wife's just a tad jealous, Ray told himself.

"I understand," Rita went on, "that you have the small ammunition manufacturers here who are suddenly short of ammo. Is there some war in the back hill country that you aren't telling us about?"

"None that I heard," Becky said, with the hint of an honest frown. "However, I've been told I'm not all that up to date on the latest rumors and intel. They're shipping someone out from Earth. A Trevor Crossenshield. He's supposed to be some hot shot in the information management business and now he's to be our expert at managing what little information we have."

Ray raised an eyebrow. "Is this new news? I should have thought that with the lack of action by the pirates that the interest from Earth would be simmering down."

Becky shook her head, sending her carefully coifed short blond hair bouncing. "It was sent out here by a priority message. I understand they poured him into a high-speed courier sloop. He'll be here in a couple of days."

"Interesting," Rita said, intrigued, but not enough to be

turned from her main interest. "Now, about those ammo salesmen."

"Let me introduce you to them," Becky said, and led Ray and Rita that way.

The men were older than Ray would have expected, say mid-fifties. Becky introduced them as men who had only recently gotten back their family businesses from Unity party thugs who had confiscated them in the recent war.

"We're both glad to be running the old places again," the balding one said, "Aren't we Armand?"

"Very, Chang. General, I'm glad to meet you face to face. I'm even more glad for your orders. I have been telling President Romali that a soldier's weapon isn't really his until he's used it and used it often. It's penny wise and pound foolish to hire a soldier and then not let him practice his trade."

"I'm glad you feel that way," Ray said. "So how come you can't provide me the ammo you promised and at the price you promised?"

The two men exchanged embarrassed glances.

"Well," Chang said, "we got this rush order from a fellow who just pulled into port and needs to get back to his colony. Seems they're worried about pirate raids and really needed the ammo bad. Since he was leaving real soon and our army is here and not going any place, we kind of figured we'd meet his schedule and meet yours by working two shifts. But that means more expenses, so the ammo costs more."

The guy finished, and seemed much relieved to have spat it out. The both of them looked relieved to have said their peace.

"A contract's a contract," Rita said, and looked ready to wale full business on them.

"Hold on, honey," Ray said, something gnawing at the

back of his mind that he didn't much care for. "Who was this colonial who was in such a hurry?"

"Guy with a strange name," Chang said, rubbing nervously at his bald pate. "Constantinople Odinkaka, or something like that."

"Constantine Odinkalu," Armand said, checking his wrist unit.

"Yeah, that's right. Conny for short, he told us to call him."

"And what was his ship that was in such an all fire hurry?" Rita asked, not catching the scent that was bothering Ray so much.

"The, ah, what was it?" Chang said.

"The *Brannigan's Special Ale*, out of New Jerusalem," Armand said.

"A ship named after a drink out of New Jerusalem?" Becky, the acting ambassador asked incredulously.

"He told me it was New Jerusalem," Armand insisted.

Chang got a pained look on his face. "I thought he said it was out of New Eden?"

Rita hit her commlink. "XO, give me a check on a ship named the *Brannigan's Special Ale*. It may be out of either New Jerusalem or New Eden."

"An ale ship out of Jerusalem?" came back with the usual ration of disbelief.

"Just tell me about it," Rita said, "Oh, and its last port of departure."

There was only a moment's pause before the XO was back. "I got a *Brannigan's Special Ale* out of New Eden. Its last port of departure was New Hebrides, skipper."

For a moment, both Rita and Ray stared at the overhead before they both said, "That's on the other side of human space."

"And a long way from here," Rita added.

"You telling me we just sold two hundred tons of ammo, mortar rounds, and grenades to a false flag?" Armand said.

"Didn't you check it out?" Becky demanded.

"Yeah." "Kind of," were the two answers.

"Did the check clear?" Rita said, sarcasm rampant.

The guys made a matching pair of pained expressions. "They paid in gold," Armand said.

"Gold nuggets," Chang added. "Pure gold. I had mine already melted down. Pure gold."

"They're paying for ammunition with gold nuggets?" Becky said, eyeing Rita and Ray with more dismay than curiosity.

Ray rubbed his face. It had been a long day and it looked to be an even longer night. "What else did this *Special Ale* barge take on? Two hundred tons of ammo is no big load."

"XO, get in touch with the port captain. What other cargo did the *BSA* take on?"

"I was already working that end of the problem, skipper. He says they cross-loaded ten thousand tons of canned meats, as well as olive oil, flour, corn and beans. There was also nearly five thousand tons of whiskies and rum."

Ray eyed Rita. "What colony can afford to pay for ten thousand tons of canned meat and half that much of hard alcohol? I think we've found where our pirates have been. Somewhere out there a gold rush is going on."

"But what kind of gold mining needs two hundred tons of small arms munitions?" Rita shot back.

"Oh, shit," Ray said.

In present company, there was no way he'd mention the alien problem. The two munitions men eyed them dumbly. The way Becky's eyes grew wide told Ray he was keeping nothing back from that woman.

"Downstairs. Now." Becky snapped.

A few moments later, Ray found himself sharing the tight confines of the embassy's secure room with two beautiful women. He saw that his wife was seated first, then arranged his chair at her elbow.

Across from them, Becky spoke first. "I know about the missing ships and the likelihood that the deep search exploration ships have fallen prey to aliens. Do you think this gold came from an alien treasure chest and the ammo is meant to keep it flowing?"

"I don't know anything," Ray said, "but I sure know I'm scared that you're more right than wrong."

"Yeah," Rita said.

"So, what do we do about it?" Becky said.

Rita tapped her commlink. It didn't work. She eyed Becky, who was up from her chair and ducking her head out the no-longer locked door. She said a few words, then glanced back in the room. "Try your call again."

A moment later, Rita was talking to her XO. "Is the *Brannigan's Special Ale* still docked at the station?"

"No ma'am. It's nearing Delta Jump out of here. I'm told Delta isn't used that much. It goes out beyond the rim."

"XO, prepare to get underway. As soon as I can get back aboard, I want us away from the pier. Alert the rest of the squadron. Tell them the same. Oh, and tell Captain Umboto that she and the *Patton* are invited along if she can get that building of hers away from the pier. Oh, and dispatch the same message to the *Northampton*. She can chase us down whenever she gets the message."

"I'm on it, skipper. Now, if you'll excuse me, I got a lot of work to do," and the XO clicked off.

Ray was only dimly aware of his wife's conversation.

He'd used the time to make his own call. "Trouble, I need my battalion of Guard back. We're heading out."

"General, I'm mighty sorry, but your Guard battalion is out on night maneuvers with my worst regiment. I can wait until they show up at first light, or I can try and chase them down and maybe get them all back together by noon tomorrow."

"I need a battalion, Trouble,"

"I got a good one. First of the first, Savannah's best."

"Get them moving up to the station and aboard ship within the hour.

"Boots and saddles," Trouble shouted to someone off net and also clicked off.

"Are you going looking for a fight?" Becky asked.

"I'm not going looking for anything," Ray said, "but I am loading up to handle any cranky bear I end up rousing out of bed."

"I'm going, too. There's got to be some adult supervision for you eager-to-blow-shit-up types."

"We're not eager, but cautious," Ray said. "And ready."

"If you really are heading out where there may be pirates, aliens, dragons, or who knows what, I'm going, too."

"Pack your cast iron underwear," Rita said. "You're going to need it at high gee."

22

A cting Captain Constantine Odinkatu breathed a sigh of relief as the newly repapered *Brannigan's Special Ale* got away from the station with over twenty thousand tons of food and drink. He wished he had more ammunition to show for his trip, but he likely had every bullet that wasn't in the actual possession of the new Savannah Army.

Beside him, Captain Grace O'Malley drummed the fingers of her good hand on the arm of the command chair she sat in. After all, he was only an acting pirate captain.

She was the real thing.

"Well, we got out of that cat convention," she muttered.

"I thought all was lost when those cruisers from Ward-haven showed up," Conny admitted.

"And you'd have run for the jump with your gold handed out and your ship empty," she reminded him.

He made no reply. After all, she was the real pirate, he was just a front man, at best. At worst? Well, he didn't want to go there again.

The cruise for Delta Jump went smoothly. Grace

O'Malley kept the main screen split in half. One side looked at the jump ahead. The other side showed the space station behind.

For the longest time, neither showed any change.

"Skipper, there's a lot of shuttle activity at the station," the woman on sensors, loaned from Grace's *Happy Highway Wench*, reported when they were still hours away from the jump.

"Two-way?" Grace asked.

"No, skipper. Most of it's from the planet to the station."

"That's not good. Reactor, can you get us more than this .9 gee?"

"I can, skipper, but I can't tell you for how long. These engines are not in the best of shape."

"Well, stand by. Once we go through the jump, I want anything extra you can give me."

"I'll get ready for it, Captain."

"See that you do," Grace muttered, but only after she'd killed her commlink.

"Maybe all that activity at the station has nothing to do with us." Conny said.

"And maybe pigs will learn to fly, me bucko," Grace said. "If I've learned anything since we let that crazy Billy Maynard talk us into this, it's that we need to thank God that there are two kinds of luck. Good luck and bad luck, cause without bad luck, we wouldn't have any at all."

"Is it that bad on the gold planet?" Conny asked. Grace had been reticent about what had happened out there.

Her quiet had been scary enough.

Her talking was getting Conny really scared.

"We told you we needed more ammo, Conny, didn't we? We risked taking this tub back to Savannah, didn't we? Of course it's a fucking mess."

Conny distanced himself from the pirate captain. He tried to stay away from the pirates when they were drunk or mad. From the smell of Grace's breath, she was both.

They were on final approach to the jump when sensors announced, "Ships are pulling away from the station. Two, three, four, five."

"Five!" Grace said.

"Five. All four of the Wardhaven ships and that Society cruiser that had been tied up to the pier so long that they were threatening to give it a street number."

"Oh, shit," Grace said.

They edged through the jump.

"Reactors, I need all you got," Grace half-shouted. "The next jump isn't all that far away. With luck, we can make it through it before they show up. Let them eat vacuum."

The bridge crew gave the pirate skipper a nervous cheer.

23

M ajor General Ray Longknife watched his wife as she slowly took the *Astute* through the jump. The jump went smoothly.

There was no ship in the system.

Slowly, more ships joined the *Astute*. All three of her sister ships were followed by the *Patton*. That all four of the Astutes were here was something of a major miracle.

"Dan, I thought you told me the *Artful* had a bum magnetohydrodynamic track," Rita had responded when Dan reported his ship ready to answer all bells.

"One's bad. But the other two are just fine. Guns and Engineering both swear they can take it apart and put it back together before we get in a fight."

"I don't know when we'll get in a fight, if ever. How come your Guns thinks she knows?"

"You know what I mean," Dan Taussig said.

"I know what you want," Rita answered. "You be careful. You're ready to make full speed?"

"Any time you order it."

Some fools were way too eager, Ray thought.

But he couldn't complain. He had his own eager beavers to deal with. The 1st of the 1st, Savannah Light Infantry, marched aboard with a will, right behind their brigadier, Trouble.

"What are you doing here, old man?" Ray demanded.

"What kind of a question is that, coming from a tooth-less old carcass like you?"

They exchanged salutes and Ray told Trouble he had room for one company on each cruiser. Trouble turned to the commander of the battalion and ordered him to distribute his men.

"Why are you really here?" Ray asked when they were alone.

"They're green, Ray," Trouble said. "They'll shake down well, but they worship the ground you walk on, old man. I figured they could use someone between them and that warrior god."

Ray had listened to his erstwhile subordinate, not sure how to take to the man Trouble was reflecting back at him. He didn't think he was rough on green troops.

Then again, it had been a while since he'd had to break in a fresh bunch from top to bottom.

And he hadn't brought all that much of the 2nd Guard Brigade back from that nameless rock.

Ray shrugged, it would be good to have another general to share some jokes with, even if he wasn't sure how he'd take to having his commands filtered through some bleeding heart Earthy scum who'd kicked his butt the last time they'd met across a battlefield.

"Jump," Rita snapped, "how many jumps out of here?"

"Three, skipper, but only one that that skunk could have ducked out of in the time they had, assuming they didn't ratchet that wreck up to two gees."

"Then, jump! Give me a course for the nearest jump."

"Helm, here, I have a course."

"Take us there, Helm."

"On our way at one gee, Captain."

"Make it 1.25 gees, helm."

"Engineering answers to 1.25 gees, ma'am. We are accelerating at 1.25 gees," and Ray found himself getting heavier. He had been standing behind his wife's command chair, there being no spare seats on the bridge. Not that there wasn't room for a few kibitzing slots on the bridge of a heavy cruiser.

The damn place was so much bigger than the close, should he say, intimate, cockpit of Rita's last transport that you hardly believed it was a ship going anyplace.

Hell, am I waxing nostalgic for the mess we were in, what was it, eighteen, twenty months ago? I need to have my head examined.

No doubt, the doc would think he was there to talk about his sudden urge, at a comfortable middle age, to go chasing off after heavily armed pirates with just a battalion behind him.

Fool doctor. That was the fun part of life.

It was all the budgets and meeting that were driving him crazy.

Oh, and standing around on a bridge, listening to his arches fall as his wife raised his weight by some twenty-plus kilos.

"You going to have business for us?" Becky Graven said, coming on the bridge. Right behind her was a rather pregnant young woman.

"Ruth, what are you doing here?" Trouble demanded of his wife.

"You got anyone else here authorized to arrest miscreants?" she shot right back at the Marine.

"But you told me . . ." got cut off.

"You told me we'd just be drilling green troops, as I recall, that night you sweet-talked me into this," she said with a wave at her swelling belly. "That there'd be no more bad guys to chase after."

"But . . ."

"No buts about it, Marine. Unless you plan to kill all the bad guys, you're going to need someone with a badge who can arrest the survivors and see that enough evidence is collected to stand up in a court of law. That's my job. Okay?" was not a question.

For someone who regularly won battles against impossible odds, watching the Marine lose one to his wife was almost comical.

Except Rita was eyeing him with a clear message to keep out of this and let Ruth stand on her own two pregnant feet.

Ray nodded submission to his own big dog.

"I'll get you a room in the most hardened section of the ship," Rita said.

"May I have the next one over?" the ambassador asked.

"Certainly, ma'am." Rita said, and the women left to look into feminine things, leaving Ray and Trouble to head for the coffee urn in the wardroom to discuss and cuss how men of such successful military careers could be put to rout by the other half of the human race. The ones with no balls.

No *obvious* balls.

But they were all back on the bridge as they slipped through the next jump.

"Damn," was not the comment you wanted to hear from sensors. Even if it was little more than a whisper.

"Tell me the bad news," Rita demanded.

"There's no ship here, skipper. There are three jumps in the system. One's doesn't matter; it's way over on the other side of the sun. However, the other two, Captain, you could easily reach either of them at one gee in the time it took us to get here, but they're in different directions." The gal at sensors flew both her hands across her chest going in directly opposite directions.

"Damn," Rita muttered, wishing the *Northampton* was right behind her, not still somewhere behind her playing catch up.

24

Commodore Rita Nuu-Longknife did her best to keep her face blank. She regretted the one explicative that had slipped out. A captain must be a rock for her crew to draw steadiness from.

Still, there were two holes that damn pirate could hide in. And Rita was more and more sure this was someone with a bad conscience doing everything he could to avoid a conversation with the powers of good.

There was no two ways about it, she'd have to split up her tiny squadron. "Dan, what kind of shape are the *Artful's* engineering spaces in?" Being a guy under the Navy scheme of things, and not having been limited to transports, he was senior officer present. Rita, however, had used her political connections to trump the old boys club and had taken command of the squadron she'd raised the money and political will for.

No way would she give up command of her squadron. However, if she had to split it up into divisions, Dan had seniority.

"Not as good as I'd like them to be," he admitted. "But we're keeping up with fleet speeds. Why, Commodore?"

Rita liked him using the commodore handle. "As Sensors has no doubt told you, we got two jumps out of here that pirate may have grabbed. Bitch is, they're about as far from each other as they can be. If we had the *Northampton* and its sniffers, we might know which one has the damn pea hiding under it, but we don't."

"So you go one way and I go the other, huh?"

"Two ships right, two ships left."

"Thanks, Commodore, I'm glad not to be heading out alone."

"Which one do you want me to go for?" Captain Izzy Umboto asked.

Exactly how the chain of command worked here, was subject to what you considered the proper relationship between old Earth and her Society of Humanity, and the outer colonies and their recent induction into said Society. Since Wardhaven had built the ships and was paying the crew's wages, Rita tended to think of them as hers. In theory, Izzy had been a captain in the Society Navy long before any of the Wardhaven officers.

Hell, they had all fought in the war on the side that fought the Society.

"If you don't mind," Rita said, "I'd like you to follow me. I've got the ambassador and the Alcohol, Drug and Explosives Enforcement Agent on board."

"It seems to me that some might consider that a case for me going the other way," Izzy said.

"You want to?" Rita asked.

"Nope, if you want me with you, and are betting you're guessing right, I'm right behind you."

"If Don wins the toss, he'll have to send one ship back to get us. If we do, I'll have to do the same," Rita said.

"It sounds to me like you're kind of cautious about taking on this pack of dogs."

"Twenty, twenty-five ships left Savannah with White-bred, or so I was told. How many Daring class light cruisers do you want to take on with a pair of Astute class cruisers?"

"Point well-taken. Am I the one that gets to run for help?"

"You're the one with the 6-inch lasers."

"I'm gonna have to do something about that," Izzy was heard to mutter.

The ships split up, and went to two gees. The *Astute* and its sisters had been fitted out on a shoe string. What that meant was that they had about half the high gee stations they needed. Rita ordered half her crew to bed.

"You going to stay up here?" Ray asked.

"Yes."

"I don't have a high gee station."

"None of you gravel crunchers do."

"So you're ordering me to bed?"

"It kind of looks that way."

"Alone?"

"I assure you, at double our weight, neither one of us could dare to be on bottom."

"There are other options. I got this nifty book called the *Kama Sutra* or something."

"To bed, Ray Longknife."

"Going, going, Commodore slave driver."

Rita got lucky. The putative pirate was halfway across the next system when they ducked through the jump. She sent the *Alacrity* back through to set a buoy to alert Dan and his division to come join them, then judging the *Brannigan's*

Special Ale to be making about one gee, she took off after her at the same acceleration.

Rita did send orders for the *Ale* to drop her acceleration and provide her papers for review.

The freighter kept running and sent back not a word.

The *Alacrity* came back through the jump and set an acceleration that would have her pulling up alongside the *Astute* and *Patton* about the time they flipped ship and started deceleration for the jump point.

An hour later, the jump buoy came through with a message that Dan had found nothing and, as they no doubt had guessed by now, was heading for their jump at 2.5 gees.

The jump master assumed that if the other division could hold that acceleration, they'd be joining up with Rita about the time they arrived at the next jump point.

Ray thanked Rita for going to one gee and got Trouble and his troopers out hiking the ship's corridors and doing what training they could.

He thanked her much more personally that evening.

The stern chase might be boring and slow, but it had some advantages.

For some.

Becky and Ruth were sharing a table in the wardroom when Rita and Ray came in the next morning. Trouble was nowhere to be seen.

After taking her own tray through the chow line, Rita joined the other women. Ray being a man of great daring, with no sense of self-preservation, joined them.

"Thank you very much for cutting the acceleration to something I can stand," Ruth said.

"You volunteered for this," Becky said. Rita noted the lack of a ring on her finger. So there was one unmarried woman at the table.

"Tell me about it," Ruth said. "I didn't think this little darling could be all that much of a problem, but I hadn't counted on it doubling in weight from one moment to the next. Or the rest of my innards doubling with it."

"Last trip out, I was still nursing," Rita said. "I held the acceleration to 1.25 gees, but these still hurt like hell," she said, waving at her breasts.

"These aren't going to quit hurting any time soon?" Ruth said, frowning down at the breasts straining at her shirt.

Rita shook her head dolefully.

"You took your nursing child out on a warship?" Becky said, her incredulity was not softened by even the tiniest bit of diplomatic tact.

"I raised the money to commission and fit out a cruiser. I was damned if I'd let some man command it. I was relegated to the transport fleet in the war. If I was doing all the scat work to get a ship away from the pier, I was going to be walking its bridge."

"Is that normal?" Becky said, and seemed to be angling the question toward Ray.

"No," he said, and quickly added, "but there is nothing normal about my wife, now is there, hon?"

"I'd rate that a 6.0 save, I would," Ruth said, writing the numbers in the air.

"Five point four in my book," Rita said, but couldn't keep her frown from turning into a soft smile.

"Things have changed a lot since the war ended," Ray said. "Some of us remember when this was supposed to be just an Exploration Service. It being the new kid on the block, it didn't have an old boys network, and my wife did a very good job of seeing that it wasn't getting one. Then along came these pirates and our scout cruisers were all that was available. And now there seems to be something else out there."

"Something else?" Ruth said, then adjusted herself in her seat to attempt more comfort. From the look on her face, she failed.

"She doesn't know?" Becky said.

"Know what?" Ruth said, irritation now blooming.

"Did your husband try to keep you from following his ship's movement?" Rita asked.

"Yeah. I've heard all that bull pucky before. I was the contract hydroponic farmer on the *Patton*. Who knows, maybe I still am. I've logged plenty of time in space."

"Ever chased pirates?" Ray asked.

"Wrong question, love," Rita said.

"I was captured by slavers," Ruth snapped. "Not once, but twice. That's how I met that lunkhead of a Marine. I woke up chained to him, not just once, but twice. Worse luck, I started to like it and so did he, it seems. Anyway, I've arrested drug lords and slavers. I figured I was about due for a pirate or two."

"How about aliens?" Ray asked.

That caused a pause in the conversation.

Ruth put down the banana she'd been eating. "Aliens?"

All three nodded.

"As in bug-eyed monster aliens?"

"No, these are more like four eyes, four arms, four legs aliens," Rita said.

Ruth leaned back in her chair and patted her stomach.

"You know, baby, Daddy might have won the argument if he'd played that card."

"He didn't?" Ray asked.

"Operation Security," Becky said. "Isn't that what you folks call it?"

Ruth shook her head. "I'm never gonna live this one down."

"You going to stay home next time?" Becky asked the gestating one.

Ruth slowly rubbed her belly. "That will depend."

"On what?" Ray ventured to ask.

"A lot of things," was clearly a cut off.

"So, how's this pirate chasing going?" Becky asked Rita, changing the subject.

"We should be back into one squadron when we do the next jump," Rita said. "As to what we do then, it depends on a lot of things," she said, eyeing Ruth.

The women enjoyed a laugh.

Ray finished his meal and stood. "I think I'll go look for someone to discuss blowing shit up with. It seems like a safer way to spend the morning."

And the women enjoyed a second laugh.

25

"How are we going to get those ships off our tail?" Constantine said. He struggled to avoid sounding like he was whining. He didn't sound successful even to his own ears.

"Maybe we don't," Captain Grace O'Malley said, using a stylus to scratch the skin inside her cast. "Damn that itches."

"But if we don't lose them, we'll lead them right back to . . ." Conny ran out of words. What exactly were they? Pirate lair? Colony? She couldn't let the Navy cruisers chase them all the way back to the gold planet.

Captain Ed Lehrer would have their heads if they let those Navy ships do that. Assuming the Navy didn't blow them out of space or shoot them first. Maybe hang them second.

Constantine didn't like not knowing what was about to happen next. He'd been feeling like that a lot since he fled Savannah. But that was nothing compared to this.

"Pull up your big girl panties, Conny. On you, they don't look so good puddled at your ankles," Grace said.

Constantine took two step backs from the pirate captain.

He did not like the look in her eyes. "Okay, what are you going to do? You're the captain."

"And you're not, so quit bothering me," she snapped at him.

He took two more steps back and found his back against the bridge wall. He studied her as she eyed the star chart she'd made the front screen into.

She tapped the commlink on her command chair. "Reactors, can you keep this up for another two days?"

"Your guess is as good as mine," came back at her.

"Any chance we could go to 1.15 tomorrow?"

"There's a chance for anything, boss. Hell, tomorrow I could learn to sing."

"God protect us from your practicing," the guy in the jump master's chair said, but he whispered it softly. Reactor and him had a thing going.

"Okay, the next jump takes us to LeMonte. We need to get out of that system fast. You think you might give me some extra gees."

"I can try, dear. Nothing beats that but a failure."

"We'll try that then."

"You're not going to drop me off at LeMonte," Constantine said, coming forward again.

"Not very likely."

"But I'm the acting captain."

"So, we can make someone else acting captain. Likely we'd better make him First President. Those are Wardhaven ships behind us. They'd like something with a democratic or capitalistic tinge to it. Not too capitalistic. That might sound like pirates or something."

The bridge crew enjoyed a chuckle.

Constantine didn't. "But those ships. They'll want to see me. I'm the one who bought all those things. Food. Great canned hams. All that ammo. You need for me to be down there to talk to them."

"He's got a point," the jump master put in.

"Yeah," Grace said, "they might want to talk to you." She pulled her dirk from her belt and tapped the point on her cast.

It looked wicked sharp.

"Some Second President might just have to report that you got killed when some crates of delicious canned hams fell over on you."

She smiled at him. At least her lips spread apart. All Constantine saw were teeth.

He fled the bridge. Behind him, there was a lot of loud laughter.

He was fighting back tears as he reached his stateroom. Once in, he locked the door. He threw himself on the bed, then realized that the flimsy door would hardly hold back a strong shoulder.

"Lights. Out," he said, and huddled in the dark.

26

C aptain Rita Nuu-Longknife studied the system before her. Exactly why had she not tried to close the distance between the freighter and her squadron?

Clearly, it had been a mistake.

Rita had assumed she'd have more time to weigh her options. Now it didn't look that way.

Ahead of her was a planet. Along its rim they could clearly make out the blue of an atmosphere.

In its orbit was a space station with one lone ship.

The ship squawked as the *Brannigan's Special Ale*.

"But ma'am," Sensors reported, "its reactors are cold and so are its engines. No ship that's been rid hard and put away wet cools that much that fast."

"What about jumps out of here?"

"Four of them, ma'am. Two are equally distant from here and close enough that the ship we've been chasing could have ducked through them."

"Could any ship that went through the dirty jumps that wrecked the sniffer have gotten here?" Ray asked before Rita could. Rita tossed him a nasty look for taking one of her prerogatives on her own bridge.

He tossed a light shrug back.

"Yes, ma'am. This is about the fastest set of jumps between here and Savannah. If you were going to intercept the colonial convoy to New Pusan, that other route would be faster. There are other, longer routes as well between here and Savannah, ma'am."

"So why take the most direct route this time?" Becky Graven asked.

"Maybe someone really needs that food and ammo," Ray answered softly.

"On that, I would bet money," Rita said, just as softly.

"So why rush back to here and just sit in orbit?" Rita asked no one. "Are there any shuttles dropping down from the station to the planet?"

"No ma'am," Sensors responded.

"So," Ray said. "Do you ask them what's going on? And if they answer, will you believe them?"

"That is the question?" Rita said, slowly. "Do I concentrate on the planet, with the whole squadron and maybe get the answers I've been looking for. Or do I split the squadron up again and go chasing after a ship that might, no matter how unlikely, be swinging around that station?" Rita spoke half to herself, half to Ray.

Ray shrugged. "Did splitting the squadron work all that well last time?"

They both knew the answer to that. And they were out well beyond the rim of human space where scout ships were disappearing. Did she really want to split her few ships up three different ways to cover the jumps and the planet?

Rita knew her next decision might well be one she'd

regret the rest of her life. Win, lose or draw, she made her call.

"Inform the squadron to follow me to the planet. Communications, let's start talking to them, shall we?"

It took only a moment for Rita to get a series of questions headed toward the planet. No doubt, the answer would be a while in coming.

When it arrived, it left Rita scratching her head.

"Hello, Commodore Rita Nuu-Longknife of the *Astute*. I have the honor of being Second President Hong Ki Jin of the peaceful and harmonious colony LeMonte," a thin, white haired and bearded oriental man said with a bow from the waist. "I regret that I cannot bring First President Constantine to the commlink. He was helping with the unloading of food from the *Brannigan's Special Ale* yesterday and a load of tinned meats fell on him, killing him instantly. I hope I can be as helpful to you as he would have wanted to be."

The smile accompanying this doleful admission was as sincere as any Rita had ever seen bought at a five and dime store back on Wardhaven.

But what it might have lacked in honest sincerity, it made up for with adamant intent.

It's my story and I'm sticking to it was, no doubt, solidly set in Mr. Hong's mind.

Then again, it might be the truth.

"The food was needed for the colony. We had a shortfall in our initial planting. As for the ammunition," the man shrugged, "you will excuse me if I do not discuss the defenses of our proud colony on an open channel. We do not know who may be listening, and, if you will excuse me for saying, we have only your word that you represent a legitimate government. Until I can see your papers, I must be cautious."

And the screen froze on an unctuous smile.

"Off net," Rita said, and the image vanished.

Becky Graven, the peripatetic ambassador, came to stand beside Rita, on the side away from Ray, she was glad to note. "That man was Earth-born or my ear has gone tin on me," she said.

"Computer, analyze the pattern of speech of last transmission. Evaluate accent and place its likely origin," Rita ordered.

"The speaker is 99.64 percent likely from Earth with a 98.32 percent likelihood that his nationality is of the Korean peninsula within one hundred kilometers of Wonsan."

"Could we have found our missing colonists from Far Pusan?" Ray asked.

"That seems likely," Rita agreed.

"But if that guy was kidnaped," Becky said, "why isn't he hollering for help?"

That left the bridge team silent.

"Maybe he likes the farm land," came on net in Ruth Tordon's voice. "I hope you don't mind that I was following matters on the bridge, but with things like they are, I don't want to be too far from a bed or the head."

"No," Rita said, "feel free to lurk on any net . . . and lurk near any creature comforts my ship can offer. Remember, I was where you are not so very long ago."

"Well, if you really are dealing with farmers like my old man, assuming the land is good and things like the government can be managed decently, I'm pretty sure you couldn't blast him off his farm with dynamite."

The three on the bridge eyed each other.

"You notice there was no mention of Whitebred. Do you think our pirate king has met with a bit of regicide?" Ray said, not at all troubled by the thought.

Rita eyed the screen. It now showed the planet they were headed toward. A basic space station orbited the planet with a lone ship.

"Where's the rest of the fleet that left with Whitebred?" she finally said. "Where's the rest of the pirates? Do I dare split up my squadron to go chasing after them, and maybe find a bear with not much more than a rabbit trap?"

Rita knew what she would have done as a brash young transport pilot. But she'd been shot out of space once and damn near killed, though she survived to grow older . . . and maybe wiser. She'd help her husband get in to see President Urm on a suicide mission, and survived. She had a husband she loved and a kid to return to.

"Maintain course and acceleration," Rita ordered. "Madame Ambassador, if you would help me come up with a second list of questions for Second President Hong, I would be very grateful. Ray, don't you have some troopers that would love to hike about my ship, or train, or something. If we're headed for a fight to recover two hundred tons of munitions, I sure want the guys behind you sharp."

And those around her moved to do her bidding.

27

"Mr. Hong, I am so glad you could meet with us," Commodore Rita Nuu-Longknife said as the Second President, now wearing a lovely long green overcoat above baggy trousers, bowed to her aboard the space station.

"It is my honor, and pleasure to be at your service. How may I help you?" he said, backing up the pier.

Rita hoped he intended his words, but she could not help but note how empty the station was.

"Your colony is not registered with the Society of Humanity," she said, as casually as she could. "I was surprised to find you out here."

"No doubt we were a surprise," the Second President said, rising to his full stature, a good five inches shorter than Rita. Ray towered over the fellow, but since the general was walking behind Rita, Mr. Hong did not seem to notice . . . or mind.

"I hope you will understand, a new colony is a very expensive thing to begin, Commodore."

Rita sported the four stripes of a captain, but Mr. Hong

was either unaware of her true rank, or had chosen to use the rank she had claimed in her introduction.

"There are officials to bribe, or should I say fees to pay, and assessments on top of those. We are but a humble people from an Earth that is little more than bread and circuses for those who have the franchise and will vote for the old crook or the new crook. For those of us who labor in the fields and have no say, it is back-breaking and heart-breaking, and may I say, soul-breaking. We chose to leave all that behind us and strike out on our own, to succeed or die by the work of our own hands."

The man spoke as if Rita should feel honored to be talking to someone of such commitment. Rita checked to see that her wallet was still in her pocket, so to speak, and dialed her sympathetic responses way down.

"So how did you manage all this?" Rita said, "A space station, no less."

"This poor thing," the politician said, indicating the station with a sweep of his hand. "We were offered it at a very low price when a client, after ordering it, chose to trade up to a larger one. We were able to use the station as the transportation out here for most of us. A most uncomfortable situation. The *Ale* was the only ship we could manage to acquire. It has served us, but only barely, and I am not at all sure it will serve us much more. Possibly, your discovery of us is to our mutual advantage. While we are making do rather well so far, no doubt there will be a need to trade in our future that we may need assistance to arrange."

"You just shipped in fifteen thousand tons of food," Ray put in from behind Rita.

"Yes, our first crop is now harvested. We are not yet willing to slaughter our pigs, so while they grow and give us more piglets, the canned hams were dearly needed, if far too dearly obtained. Poor Constantine."

Yes, poor Constantine who isn't here to answer any questions, Rita thought, but said, "Do you mind if some of my crew take a look at the *Brannigan's Special Ale?*"

"As a matter of fact, I do," Hong said, and looked so sad to be disagreeing. "It is our ship and its condition shall remain a trade secret. However, I can give you access to its full log, both of the trip out here from Earth and its latest voyage to, what was it, Savannah, am I correct?"

"Savannah," Rita agreed.

And that was how every conversation with Mr. Hong, the Second President, went. Effusively sincere, but reluctantly unhelpful. Ray did get to drop some of his troops down to get in some dirt work.

What Trouble reported back was a colony reduced to basics: dirt trails, log buildings and outhouses out back with not much else in front. Still, the farmers were happy as they put in one crop or harvested another. Everyone Trouble and his troopers talked to was happy to be here. Those that knew anything about their government, and they were few, had nothing but praise for it.

"That sound too good to be true?" Rita asked Trouble over the net.

"No way I'd dispute that with you, Commodore."

"Have you heard anything about Admiral Whitebred?" Ray put in.

"I ask, General. All I get are blank stares, even from the ones that admit to knowing they have a Second President named Hong. Name recognition for politicians is pretty slim down here."

"That will be their problem, come election time," Becky said, dryly.

"But what is it for us now?" Rita said. Something was gnawing at her. She did not like the feel of it.

"I think we've got a brick wall here, Rita," Ray said softly.

"Yeah," she agreed. "Trouble, recover back aboard."

"On our way, ma'am."

"XO, advise the squadron. We sortie tomorrow at 0900."

"On it, skipper."

Rita turned to Ray, and they slowly walked back to their quarters.

"Ray, I think I have made a major mistake."

"In what way, Dear?" he said, listening, really listening to her with his ears, eyes and whole face.

"I should have split up the squadron and continued the pursuit of that ship."

Ray nodded. "But you had that ship in port. And you and I both know that dividing your forces is never a good idea. Somewhere out here are twenty plus pirate ships. And who knows what firepower the alien ships have that are making our scout vanish? That's the bitch about war, Honey. You make your choice. Sometimes it's right. Sometimes it's wrong. You never know, and dear God, there's no such thing as a do-over."

Somewhere in that, Ray closed the door to their quarters. Somewhere in that, Rita folded herself into Ray's strong arms.

"I know all that, you big galoot," she said to his chest. "It's just I think I've just made the worst mistake of my life. And a horrible mistake for all humanity."

"I hope we haven't," Ray said.

That was not the support Rita needed. Still, it was all she was likely to get today.

Only tomorrow would tell her if her worst nightmare was about to come true.

28

Captain Ed Lehrer was relieved to hear that the *Happy Highway Wench* was back in system and leading a ship claiming to be the *Brannigan's Special Ale* towards a quick orbit. He was dirtside, as he had been for too much of the time since Grace left.

It wasn't just to see her smiling face that had him there when her shuttle grounded on the sand beneath the fort. He was hungry.

"How'd it go?" he asked her as she strutted from the shuttle. "How's your arm?" he appended when he realized the cast was gone, but the arm was still in a brightly colored sling that he'd mistaken for just her usually flamboyant dress.

"Things went better than my arm is doing. I don't think I'll be slapping anyone silly with it anytime soon, if ever." She turned as boys started lugging crates marked Canned Meat and sacks of potatoes from the shuttle.

"I got what you sent me for," she said, one hand resting proudly on her hip.

"And ammo?"

Two men came out with a large box slung between them. Stenciled on it were the identifiers for military grade rifle ammo.

"Calico Jack will so be glad to see that," Ed said. "We've about shot ourselves dry."

"Things been that bad?"

Ed scowled as he nodded. "Worse. We thought all those crates up at the mine were their food. It turns out a lot of them were explosives. We didn't notice until quite a few of them had walked away after midnight. We stopped that once we knew it, but we've been getting a lot of those mining explosives thrown back at us."

He and Grace started the walk back into town as a second shuttle dropped into the bay in a spray of water that left the air laden with the smell of salt water.

"The food's been tight. There's stuff we can eat, but going into the jungle to find it is worth your life. We probe at them. They probe at us. It seems every day there's more dead. Some of us. Some of them. It never ends."

"Don't they know when to give up?" Grace asked.

"And if any of them did, how'd we know they had? We had the big fellows with us for a week or two, wasn't it? How many words of their jabber did you catch?"

Grace shrugged, then winced. "If they motioned to their beak with one of their hands, I took it that they were thirsty or hungry. Of the noise coming out of that beak, your guess was as good as mine."

"Yeah, so we kill them and they kill us, and in between we've mined some good silver and panned some nice gold. By the way, how'd the exchange of gold for goods go? Anyone give you any trouble?"

Grace laughed. "Anyone turn down gold nuggets you mean?"

"Stupid question, huh?"

"Very stupid."

"Did you have any trouble? I was worried you'd be followed back."

"I was followed, but I lost them at LeMonte."

"They found LeMonte?"

"They found a nice unregistered colony at LeMonte with a lot of happy people saying nice things about their life and 'I don't know nothin' about no pirates, ma'am'."

"Did that really work?"

"I lost my tail at LeMonte and I didn't see hide nor hair of them since."

They arrived at the Captains' table ahead of a batch of boys carrying food and ammo. Captains were waiting for them. More arrived when jugs of rum started clinking.

"We got plenty for everyone. There's more down by the landing," Grace shouted for the captains, and the pirates lurking in the shadows. Those lurking included a lot of the farmers as well.

Lots of them took off for the shuttle landing.

"Calico Jack will have to make sure some reliable sentries are posted," Ed said, and stepped out to find Jack and make the arrangements. That done, he and Calico rejoined Grace.

She was eyeing the captains as they swilled their preferred drink while the hams roasted over an open fire and the potatoes baked.

"We're missing a few captains, aren't we?"

"Yeah," Ed admitted. "Black Bart and Ben Hornigold took a couple of skippers out that don't much care for messing in the mud, as they said. Ben found a rug, or wall hanging or something at the last place they raided and he thinks it's a star map. Me, I think they're chasing around with a treasure map that don't show a thing, but they weren't providing all that many trigger-pullers and you couldn't count on their lasers to work if we needed them to slash and burn some jungle, so they're gone and any gold or silver we take out while they gone, they don't get a cut."

"I guess that's good," Grace said, and pulled a jug of rum from a passing kid.

Outside, a mortar woofed as a round went out.

"Calico, we got problems?" Grace asked.

"Not a one, now that you're back, honey," he said, sidling up to her and giving her a peck on the cheek. "I got ammo. We can drop a few rounds out there to let them big bastards know we're here and they ain't."

"Good," Grace said.

Then there was a huge explosion.

"Shit, that don't sound like a mortar round," Calico Jack said before Ed could.

They bolted for the door. Outside, to the left, a huge fire was raging as the roofs of several buildings and a few tents burned. As they watched, another large sack of something arched in, sputtering fuses burning. It landed on a tent and scattered flaming liquid over it and a dozen tents around it. Screaming men and women ran out, many in flames.

Some remembered to drop and roll out the fire. Most didn't. They kept running until someone knocked them down or they fell down dead and still flaming.

"To the walls," someone was shouting.

"To the walls," became the common cry.

"Oh, shit," Ed said as his commlink came to life, then he grabbed Grace with one hand, Calico with the other.

"What the hell?" Calico said.

"We got bigger trouble," Ed said. "My Number Two says Black Bart just jumped in system. He ain't heading down here, but making almost two gees for the jump to Port Elgin."

"How come?" Grace asked.

"He ain't saying, but I'll give you two guesses."

"Has he got something on his tail?" Grace demanded.

"I don't know, but I'd head for the shuttles, if I were you," Ed said.

"You do that," Calico Jack said. "I'll try to hold here. Get me more ammo."

"I'll shuttle down ammo," Grace said, "you shuttle up sailors." She turned to Ed. "You think we ought to get a ship on the other side of that jump to look around?"

"I don't know. If Bart's outrun whoever is chasing him, you want to give them a hint where to go?"

"Shit," was all Grace said.

Ed's commlink came alive again. "Ben Hornigold is back in system," he repeated the words of his Number Two for those listening. "He's also bolting for the exit, but he's hollering. Yes, they got into a fight. They lost the other two ships. He's not saying how, but they're gone, and them that got them are going hell for breakfast after them."

Ed paused. "That's it, folks."

"We got a problem," Calico Jack said.

"I'll get ammo down here so you can do a fighting retreat," Grace said. "We got to get the laser gunners back aboard, Jack. We got to if we're going to have any chance."

"With Billy Maynard and his crews, you think we'll have any chance?" Jack asked.

"I don't know, but with half our crews down here," Ed said, and left the rest of his thought to a shrug.

"Okay, get me ammo. I'll get you gunners. And yes, we got to get out of here."

Ed, gun at the ready, trotted with Grace through a burnt landscape that had once been a pleasant walk through trees swaying in the wind. Back at the beach, Grace's shuttle was already warming up reaction mass for a fast take off.

"Orbit, Gomez, and don't spare the horses," she shouted.

29

C aptain Edmon Lehrer prepared for his first space battle. Hell, except for a few skirmishes along the River of Gold, he'd never been in *any* battle.

He'd been a school teacher when the Unity party recruiters came along and offered him a better deal. Not only would there be no more grading students' papers, but he'd have a chance at all the things he'd ever dreamed of doing or having, but been too afraid to grab for.

He'd ended up as a political officer on one of the ships that never seemed to leave the pier. That suited him well. But he was curious, and he wasn't content to just check people's mail for anti-party words or thoughts. He'd actually started studying how to operate a warship.

After the war, he'd been quietly taken aside and offered a chance to command an old Daring cruiser for fun and profits, assuming he was willing to pass along a 30% cut to someone and not ask who.

He'd taken two fat freighters and brought both of them into Savannah where officials looked the other way, and made it easy to sell stuff whose bill of lading came with the ink still wet.

Ed tried to remember when he'd made up his mind to become a pirate and murder people for a living. He couldn't point to any one decision.

He'd started down a slippery slope and, then suddenly he was going full bore for the devil's ass and there was no turning back.

Now, he had a god-awful fight coming at him, assuming you could trust the hurried screams from Ben Hornigold.

Problem was, he didn't much believe anything Ben said. Not since he turned up shouting about there being gold. He'd been right about there being gold.

Not so right about how easy it would be to take it.

That worried Ed. Ben had gotten it all wrong how easy the aliens would be last time.

Now he was screaming and running for all he was worth from this new bunch of aliens.

Ed launched himself from the shuttle, caught a handle and pointed himself for the exit of the shuttle bay. In hardly a minute, he shot onto his bridge and, catching a hand-hold, aimed himself for the command chair.

Number Two vacated it seconds before he hit it.

"What's our situation?" he snapped.

"Five 6-inch lasers up, boss. Three more we're working on. What with all the crew coming back, maybe we can get two of them up. We got 6 of the 4-inch pop guns working. Two more are being worked on with a chance we can get them worth something in a fight."

"Reactors?"

"As you'd expect, ready to answer bells. She don't think we're good for more than two gees though."

"Reactors," Ed said, tapping his commlink, "I may want three gees."

"I want a nice guy with hot buns, but I settle for that pussy you got on jump."

"You living to get in the sack with that pussy may depend on three gees."

"I'll see what I can do."

Ed eyed his boards. In the war, he'd been senior political officer on a General class cruiser. They'd never been in a fight, but their boards always showed green. He'd been proud of his ship until a drunk chief explained one night that the board always showed green because they wired it to show green, not because all or even any of the systems were up.

"You jolly man, it's all a joke. We pretend to be war ready, and you pretend to win the war."

Ed had had the man whipped the next morning. He didn't tell the captain why, he just had the chief whipped at morning muster.

Ed had been promoted to the flagship the next month. No one ever asked him why he whipped that old chief, but then, no one ever shared with him again what was the truth behind the war, either.

Now, the *Queen Anne's Revenge* had better do a lot more than pretend to fight for him.

Eight hours later, the town was burning from end to end. The last shuttles were waiting on beach for the last of the ground party to make a run for them. The *Revenge* had the top cover job, no accident that.

"Ed, I need covering fire," Calico Jack called.

"We'll be here for it for the next ten minutes. Start running."

"We're running."

"Lasers, burn that town. Burn that jungle. Burn those bastards."

The *Revenge* was already nose down, facing the planet. When the forward laser batteries were expended, Ed would flip ship. He expected to do a lot of flipping ship for the next ten minutes.

"We got targets," Guns announced.

"Fire all forward batteries," Ed ordered.

Five seconds later, he had the helm flip ship. That took five seconds.

"Fire all aft batteries."

Five seconds later, the *Revenge* began to reverse again. In twenty seconds, the forward batteries were reloaded. "Fire."

Flip.

"Fire."

Flip.

For ten long minutes, they fired and flipped and fired again.

A few times, Ed felt dizzy, but on screen, he was watching Calico Jack's comm camera as the man fell back with his troops.

"First line. Fire!" A crash of volley fire.

"Fall back."

"Second line. Fire!" Some just fired a round. Others went full auto.

"Fall back, damn you, and save your ammo!" came on net.

"Third line. Fire."

"Fall Back. Don't pick up that man, you idiot. Fall back!"

Fire. Fall back. Fire. Fall back. It went on and on as the night was lit up by volley fire, exploding alien fire canisters and laser fire from the *Revenge* above.

There were other ships leading and trailing the *Revenge*

in orbit. They got off a few rounds here and there, but it was the *Revenge* that covered for Calico Jack and his troopers' withdrawal.

Now they were at the beach. A rank fired, many emptying their magazines on full auto, then raced to board a shuttle. It backed out into the bay, wheeled about and started its takeoff run.

Then the next rank fired, almost all on full automatic. It hardly took a word from Calico for them to break ranks and scuttle aboard the second to last shuttle pulled up on the beach.

It was backing out even as people were still clambering aboard. The last guy didn't make it through the door before they were wheeling around and nosing into their takeoff run.

The last rank fired, and most of them bolted for the one remaining shuttle.

But a few of them formed a short, thin line. Was that Calico Jack in the middle of them? In the night, it was hard to spot the flamboyant colors of his shirt. This solid group held for a long moment, then leveled their guns and went to full auto as they backed up toward the shuttle.

Rocks and arrows assaulted them. Some of the arrows looked as long as a man. One cut through a gunner and drove him back ten feet into the surf.

A fire bomb exploded a bit to the right of the shuttle. It began to pull off from the beach. The last of the gunners broke as their weapons bolts came open on an empty magazine.

Ed stared hard at the screen. Was Calico the last one shooting? The last one backing up, step by step?

Whoever was last, one of those long arrows took him and he was down.

"Get the hell out of here," came on net.

Either Calico was ordering the shuttle out – or that was him slumped over two meters of wood in the sand?

The shuttle backed off the beach.

In a moment, the beach was crawling with big bastards. Some threw rocks that bounced off the shuttle. Others drew back their huge bows and sent two-meter-long arrows arching out at the shuttle.

Some hit. Most appeared to glance off, but others seemed to hit and pierce through. Could they make orbit with that kind of damage?

In a moment, it didn't matter. A fire bomb hit the bow of the shuttle and showered flame all over it. Still, the shuttle pulled through the ring of fire, and picked up speed for take-off.

But something was wrong. Whether it was an arrow, or the fire, or something else, the shuttle failed to pick up speed. It taxied rather than shot off the water.

It taxied and taxied, never building up speed. In its wake, more arrows were shot into the water and more fire bombs exploded in its wake.

Watching from above, Ed spotted the problem. There was a reef off the beach. It was what protected that bay from the full fury of the ocean storms.

Usually, the shuttles were well airborne before they got close to it.

This shuttle wasn't. Behind it, vengeful arrows and fire wreathed the water. Ahead of them was a light color in the water.

The tide was high. Maybe high enough to let them get over the reef and down the coast to someplace where another shuttle could pick them up. Ed reached to tap his commlink, to warn the shuttle. To arrange something.

The shuttle hit the light water.

It began to come apart. Then the containment system on the antimatter storage unit failed catastrophically.

The explosion sent chunks of shuttle and steaming water shooting into the air.

Some of it ended back on the beach. Big bastards went down before the power humanity could unleash.

"Lasers, target the beach, if we still have a shot."

"I got three big boys and four of the little kids," gunner said, reporting on his 6-inch and 4-inch batteries.

"Turn that beach to glass, and those bastards on it."

"Done, boss," and it was.

30

———

Captain Edmon Lehrer took a few moments to regain his composure, but only a few. He had a battle ahead of him, or one fast flight. He called up his captains on net; most were just getting onto their ships' bridges and finding their seat.

Ed polled them. "Folks, we just lost Calico Jack. I don't think he'd want us to do anything stupid in his memory, so, do we wait for the big fellows to show up here, or do we run?"

"Run," came as one word from the surviving nine skippers.

"Break orbit as soon as you can, we'll join up on the run to the jump out of here," Ed said, and then turned the job over to his helm to get them moving out.

They were an hour out of orbit, with Grace and Annie forming up on his *Revenge* and the others working their way into a wide wedge when the jump point started spitting out ships.

They were big and they were round.

"Sir," Sensors reported, "I make six of them, so far. Some of them have two reactors. Some three. Two have four."

"You have any visuals?"

"No, sir. The best we have hardly show them as better than dots."

"What's their speed?"

"Like us, they came through the jump as dead slow, sir. They ain't dumb. Now, they're putting on acceleration. I make it as a bit more than one gee."

"Can they cut us off from our jump?" Ed asked.

"Not at one gee they can't, sir."

"Keep me informed."

"Ed," came in a quaking voice. It was Billy Maynard.

"I'm here, Billy."

"Do you see what I see?"

"If you mean the, ah," Ed glanced at Sensors. He held up both hands, showing eight fingers, "the eight strange ships coming at us, yeah, I see them."

"What are we going to do?"

"We?" Ed couldn't help but say.

"We're all in this together."

"Billy, you let four of your captains go wandering off freelancing around on their own treasure hunt and bringing this down around our ears. And I notice that neither of the two survivors are all that interested in talking to us about what they found and how these things followed them back. It might be nice to know what they did so we could figure out how mad these things are at us."

Though, considering how things had gone on the Planet of Gold, once these new arrivals talked to their four eyes down there, no doubt, there would be a lot of mad to go around.

"Ed, you got to help us stop them from doing to Port Elgin what we did to this place."

"I do?"

"Yeah, we split the gold. We got to split the defenses."

"I was thinking of splitting the defenses by defending LeMonte."

"Ed, you know better than that. You were in the war. If we split up, they can defeat me and then defeat you. If we got any chance, we got to do it together. One big fleet."

"Without Black Bart's cruiser."

"You know I can't make a captain go against his crew." Billy was sweating bad now. "I'll tell you what I'll do. Once we get through the next jump, I'll message the *Your Bad Day* and ask the crew to toss Bart in the clink and join up with us."

Ed knew what that was worth.

"Okay, I'll see what I can do about talking my crew into standing with you."

"Good. If we all stand together, I think we'll really have a chance."

Like they'd done with Calico Jack, Ed thought bitterly. *We didn't know what we were sticking our noses into when we landed back there. How can Billy think he knows how strong we are in a fight with what's just jumped in here?*

Ed polled his captains. The majority were for forgetting Billy and his bunch and running straight for LeMonte. The minority included Grace O'Malley and Anne Bonney.

"Those bastards aren't worth much in a fight," Grace said, "but they're better than nothing. We let the big bastards roll them up, then they'll come looking for us next. I say we make them have to take us all in one bite."

Strange how having a pair of gals showing more fight than the guys quickly changed the vote.

Ed called Billy up. "We'll fight with you, but Billy, we need one commander. This co-commander shit didn't work all that well back there."

"What do you mean, we all did what Calico Jack said to do."

Ed eyed Billy dolefully.

The other pirate captain flinched. "You want me under your command, huh?"

"Kind of. Actually, kind of like totally," Ed said.

"I'll talk it over with the boys."

"Billy, with Black Bart and Ben Hornigold running, about half of your 6-inchers are gone. If you want us in the fight for Port Elgin, as I see it, it's not us backing you up, it's you going into our fighting line."

Billy didn't look like he wanted to do that math, but Ed didn't let him wiggle off the hook.

"Okay, you command. We'll talk this over as much as we can beforehand, but when it comes to the fight, you're in charge."

They made it to the jump, with a dozen of the big fellows' ships on their tail. Three of the ships had ducked down to the planet. Shortly after they made orbit, there was some kind of radio traffic between the ships in orbit and the ships in pursuit.

No one on Ed's ships could make anything of the transmission, but suddenly the big fellows' ships cut down a bit of a gee on their deceleration. That would mean they'd have to brake even harder when the time came to pull up at the jump, but it let them close the distance faster for now.

"I don't think they liked what they saw back there," Ed said.

"Would you, if that was our people?" Grace said.

"Maybe we ought to just split and run," Billy said.

Ed had noticed Kim, the acting battle captain for the farmers, lurking on his bridge. Now he stepped forward. "Our wives and children are on Port Elgin and LeMonte. We talked about this before as we were running from the Gold planet. If you attempt to run away and leave our people to die like that, we will fight you. We are on most of your ships. You abandon us and you will have to kill every one of us on your ships. Do not make a mistake. We will not die easily."

Ed turned in his chair to face Kim. "You will be safe on my ship. We have already decided to fight."

"I know you. You were a friend of Calico Jack, and he was good to my people. I trust you. It's Billy I don't trust."

"Strange that," Grace said on net, "we don't much trust him either."

"Billy, a word from me to your captains," Ed said. "Any ship that tries to take off, like Bart and Ben did, will be shot down as it breaks away. This I swear. We fight together, or we figure out a way to all run together, but we won't leave anyone behind like Calico to die so the rest of us can run away."

Ed chose his words hard, knowing that this was a squadron of free men on free ships. If a crew voted to run, the ship would run.

He wondered if his ship would actually fire on a running ship.

He doubted he'd have any trouble getting one of his ships to fire on one of Billy's if it ran. One of their own. It was a coin toss.

On the other side of the jump, they spotted Bart and Ben running for all the gees their ship could put on. No surprise, no amount of talking would get either one of them to come back.

The pirate fleet, seventeen strong, set course for the next jump.

It didn't stay seventeen for long. The *Brannigan's Special Ale* was the first to fall out, it's engines unable to hold at 1.15 gees. Slowly it fell behind, it's small crew begging them to come back for them.

"We've got food. We've got ammo. You need us," Constantine Odinkalu alternately begged and demanded. No one was willing to put themselves at risk.

"Pick another jump, one further out in this system," Grace suggested. "Take it and see where it leads you. With luck, the big bastards won't follow you."

That at least shut them up. They headed for the farthest jump, but it didn't do them any good. One of the two reactor types of the big fellow's ships, took off after them. Ed's jump master did the math. The big fellow would catch the *Ale* before it got out of the system.

Whatever it did when it caught up with the human ship would not be observed by them, they'd be long gone into the next system.

That left sixteen against eleven.

Then the *You Made My Day*, a small converted freighter with only two 4-inch pop guns hollered that it's second reactor was overheating. They begged for shuttles to take them off now while they were still in formation. Annie Bonney explained to them that no shuttle could keep up with a fleet at 1.1 gee. If it pulled away from one ship, it would never make it to another ship accelerating at that energy.

Still, the crew begged to be allowed to get *Day* close enough to one ship so the shuttle trip would be only a quick dash.

"You get close to any of us with a faulty reactor that

could have you yawing all over the place and we'll shoot you down where you stand," Ed had to tell them.

"Won't any of you let us get close to you? Any of you with shuttles?"

The silence was deafening.

Their cursing was boring. Ed had the commlink broken with that one.

So, a second ship joined the *Brannigan's Special Ale* trying for the farthest jump.

It was fifteen to eleven as they headed into the jump.

They lost two more small ships crossing the next system. The bastards again detached a single one of their own to chase down the two wayward human ships.

Three ships fell out the next system. For the first time, one of them was Ed's.

"You keep this up, shedding us like snake skin," Captain Malmo Tarkus said, "and there won't be anything left to fight with."

"I'm sorry, Tark, but the big ships have the bigger and stronger engines," Ed said.

"What are you going to do when one of your lovely ladies with a 6-incher in her pocket cries for help?"

"The same thing he's done when you boys, with six inches in your pockets holler," Grace said.

"I'll see you in hell, lady."

"Make a run for the furthest jump, Tark. Who knows, you may get back to human space long before we do," Ed said.

Tark cut the comm before he said anything more.

It was twelve to ten at the next jump.

31

Captain Edmon Lehrer was glad they didn't lose any more ships crossing the next system. The shrunken pirate fleet was down to the three Darings and the better of the converted or captured merchant ships.

The three cruisers had more 6-inch guns up and ready than they'd had when they started this crazy hunt for gold. It was amazing what a fleet of hostiles on your ass did to the motivation and creativity of a crew.

They went through that jump at dead slow, with the big bastards not an hour behind them. In the Port Elgin system, Ed held his first council of war.

"Anybody have any idea how we fight this thing? If you do, I'm all ears."

"Let's stay here at the jump point. Shoot them as they come through," Billy suggested.

Ed's jump master was shaking his head before Billy finished.

"I've seen jumps dodge out twenty thousand klicks as you're approaching them. I've heard of jumps that jumped a hundred thousand klicks in one move. We call 'em jumps for more reasons than one, you know. Boss, what's the range of our 6-inchers?'

Ed had read the book, though he'd never actually fired at another ship. "Supposedly 24,000 klicks, but don't bet on them doing much good beyond 17,000." He paused, then added. "So, there's a good chance they could jump in beyond our best range and a long chance they could be way out of range."

"And Murphy says the worst will happen just when you don't need it," the jump master added, under his breath, but loud enough for the whole bridge to hear.

Ed took a deep breath. He knew he ought to put it up to a vote. That was the pirate way. But he could see no other way than the one he was about to order.

"Set course for Port Elgin. We'll make our stand there. Begin a 1.1 gee acceleration on my mark."

Silence roared back at him.

"Mark," he said.

We are committed.

32

"I f something doesn't happen soon," Major General Ray Longknife said, "our forces are going to melt away."

"They already are," Rita said. In this meeting, she sat at his elbow. Or maybe he sat at hers. It would be unwise of him to try to clarify that. Beck Graven provided the political insight from where she sat at Rita's elbow.

Ray hadn't failed to note how Rita always managed to sit between him and the ambassador. Was Rita protecting her turf?

On Ray's other side was the new addition to their inner group. Trevor Crossenshield was their new Chief of Intelligence. He did seem to know a lot, and had done a good job of correlating all the information flooding into Savannah about strange things, ranging from missing scout ships to a two-headed snake being seen on Hurtford.

Ray found himself wondering if that two-headed snake had any better luck deciding where to go than the rest of humanity.

Across from Ray sat Trouble and his very pregnant wife. Trouble had a division of light infantry in advanced training and another one coming up. His wife provided the law enforcement point of view.

They were still debating whether pirates should be shot on sight or offered a chance to surrender and face a trial.

Again, that two-headed snake syndrome.

"The pair of cruisers we got from Lorna Do, the *Lion* and the *Puma,* are getting ready to head back home," Rita reported. "We'll miss their 8-inch guns, but with no ships going missing and no colonies attacked . . ." Rita ended with a shrug.

"I guess they think we were shouting 'wolf'," Becky said.

"And New Eden is making noises they want their *Vampire* and *Fury* back," Rita added.

Ray eyed the screen on the wall behind his wife. It showed the four Wardhaven super heavies, like the *Astute* that they were meeting on. All five of the Ramble class scout cruisers were out now. The *Exeter* was due in soon with the *Northampton*, both 8-inch heavies. Their yard period had been extended by a strike at the Nuu docks at High Ward-haven. The post war expansion was not meeting everyone's expectations and some workers were demanding their share of it.

Ray sighed. He liked democracy much more than the dictatorship it replaced. Still, it *was* messy.

"Anybody have any idea what we do to keep our forces together?" Becky asked no one in particular.

"Do we let more folks know about the aliens out there?" came from Ruth Tordon, who was working hard at earning the nickname Mrs. Trouble. She was the latest one to learn of the aliens out there, and seemed really bothered by them.

"I want my kid to grow up," was her comeback when pushed.

"We're being looked at as the kid who cried 'pirate'," her

husband said. "Would we have any better luck hollering 'alien,' without producing a few?"

"Anyone want to dress up in an alien suit?" Crossenshield said. He didn't like to be called Crossie.

"Crossie, suggestions like that are going to make us wonder how intelligent our intelligence is," Rita said.

She'd taken an immediate dislike to the man. "Is he with us or reporting back to some cabal on Earth?" she demanded of Ray.

Ray, having no better an answer to that question than she did, had only shrugged. "Short of not inviting our intel chief to meetings, what can we do?"

Crossie got invited to all meetings, but that didn't mean Rita liked it. Or him.

Four commlinks beeped at the same time. Ray, Rita, Trouble and Crossie all tapped their wrist units.

"We got trouble," came in a three-part echo from three different sources.

Crossie's said, "Boss, you won't believe the shit we got coming in."

"Talk to me," Rita said to her communication's officer.

"Ma'am, we just had a ship jump into the system hollering all kinds of stuff that would get his comm license revoked, but the gist of it is that there are aliens right behind him. Aliens that have slaughtered human colonists."

"Is this on a public channel?" Rita asked her comm chief.

Becky nodded. "My folks have it, too. They're picking up all kinds of chatter. Uh, oh, it just broke on a news channel. Make that three. No, all of them."

Ray gave his silent intel chief a gimlet eye.

"I can verify all that," he said.

"Sensors," Rita said. "Talk to me about this new ship in system."

"We make it out to be a former Daring class cruiser. It's in pretty bad shape, maybe half of the main battery is operational. Though, considering that none of those lasers are supposed to be usable, that might not be a bad accomplishment," she said, dryly.

"Its engines are overheated. I'd say he's been running fast and long. No telling how long, though. Oh, and its course is for the Alpha Jump out of here. He's not coming to the station."

"Thanks. XO, are there any ships in system that could intercept him?"

"No, ma'am. Unless some ship comes through Alpha, we got nothing. The *Exeter* and the *Northampton* are due in tomorrow. They might catch him on the other side."

"Comm, send to that ship. Tell it to report to the station here. Tell them that if they don't come in, we will intercept them. Also, Comm, send to *Exeter*. Be on the lookout for a fast running former Daring. Apprehend it. Comm, do we know what that ship is squawking?"

"No, ma'am. They throttled their squawker before they came in system."

"That's illegal," Becky said.

"Under Society regulations," Crossenshield put in. "Out on the rim, they didn't require that."

"But we're all good members of Society now," Ray said with a grin. As the man credited with the death of President Urm and the sudden end to the Unity War with the Society, his new attitude wasn't lost on the meeting.

"Comm, send to the unidentified ship in system. Tell them that they are in violation of Society regs, having turned off their recognition repeater and will immediately come to the station so it can be repaired."

"Oh, they're going to love that, if that's a pirate ship like I'm betting," Trouble said, with a chortle.

"Brigadier, how fast can you mount up a force, and how big?" Ray said.

Trouble was all serious business as he faced Ray. "I've already put my troopers on alert, sir. The 1st regiment is ready to move out any time you can provide shuttles to lift them to the station. The 2nd and 3rd should be ready by 0600 tomorrow."

Ray turned to Rita. "How fast can you get your cruisers away from the pier?"

"My squadron is ready now, sir," she snapped. "Quarters were rather roomy for the one company you put aboard them last time. May I suggest we try for two?"

"Trouble?"

"I'd say there's room for three companies per ship, ma'am, if you got the air for us. I can have a regiment aboard as fast as you can provide lift."

"Comm here," came on Rita's link. "The *Lion* and *Puma* have reversed course and are headed back to the station. The *Rambling Gal* and *Rambling Rose* are in system and headed for the station. We're sending out recall signals to the *Rambling Road*, *Rambling Guy*, and *Rambling Star*."

"They are all within four or five jumps," Crossie put in. "Say a week or less to get here. The *Concord*, out of Wardhaven is also in that range," he added.

"Comm, send to *Concord*. 'We're throwing a party with some pirates and saving you a place close to the bar. Longknife sends'," Rita said.

Crossie was going down a list. "The *Vampire* and *Fury* from Pitt's Hope are a bit further afield."

One glance from Ray, and Rita was inviting them to the party as well.

"So," Ray said. "Do we rush out with what we have, or wait until we've got a full force?"

"That stranger came in the Delta Jump," Rita said. "That's the jump we used to chase the *Brannigan's Special Ale* through to LeMonte."

Ray grimaced. "There were a lot of nice people, but I didn't see anything like planetary defenses."

Ray breathed out, searched for his center. It was good to hit your enemy with a weighted blow. It was also good not to let a lot of civilians get murdered. He didn't have to look around the table to know that he was senior officer present.

Rita and Trouble's rank were local honors, handed out, possibly illegally, by the planets that sent them to work. His rank came straight from Earth. That honor might have been awarded for a murder he hadn't committed, but, however you counted it, it was senior rank and from a source all present had to salute.

"We go with the most we can put together as quickly as we can. Rally point for all troops and ships will be Port Elgin. Becky, can you arrange with the Savannah President for us to commandeer a couple of troop transports? Trouble, how many regiments do you have ready to move out?"

Trouble had on his war face. "Three are combat ready. Two more are able to meet ship movements with their weapons. I wouldn't count on them to maneuver under fire, but if they are dug in, they can defend."

No doubt, that defense would be a bloody affair.

"Defend is all I intend to do," Ray said.

"Then defend we will."

"Rita?"

"I'd recommend that we wait long enough for the two

cats to join us. That would give us six heavy cruisers and two light ones. Trouble can load four battalions on them. Becky, we need lift for eight battalions and support elements."

"I'll get right on it," the ambassador said, and walked over to a corner of the room where she'd likely catch less of the conversation and pass it along to the political heart of the planet beneath them.

No doubt, she would also tell tactful, diplomatic lies if necessary.

Eighteen hours later, the *Astute* led out seven heavy cruisers, and the *Patton,* along with six transports loaded with troops, drop shuttles, and supplies.

It had been a hectic time with hardly a moment to think.

Now, with the force committed, Ray had time to consider.

He'd wanted to talk to the aliens. Had he thrown that option to the wind? And a bloody wind at that?

He would know soon enough.

A cting Brigadier General Terence Tordon by name, but Trouble to everyone he knew, stood on the bridge of the *Astute* as it closed towards an orbit on the unregistered colony of LeMonte.

The planet had not answered any of the hails the fleet had sent.

Worse, Sensors reported no activity on any electronic spectrum. "There's nothing there for us to sense," she had said.

Trouble doubted he was the only one with a sick feeling in his gut.

It had started the moment they jumped into this system. Sensors had reported reactors. Plenty of them. All headed for the jump farthest from them. As their fleet jumped in, that fleet jumped out.

Not one of the reactors on those ships had a signature that matched one made anywhere in human space.

That was one question. The bigger question, however, was what had they done here? What had they left behind?

"Trouble, prepare a drop mission," Major General

Longknife said from where he stood beside his wife who sat, intently eyeing the fleet's status from her commodore's command chair.

"You might want to get your troops moving to drop stations before we go to zero gee in orbit," the commodore advised.

"Aye, aye, ma'am," Trouble said. *You could take the Marine out of the Corp, but you couldn't take the Corp out of the Marine,* he thought, and moved to implement his orders.

The drop went smoothly, as he'd expected. The bosuns on the cruiser's long boats were well trained. His two best battalions provided the troops.

There was no opposition from the ground.

There was nothing from the ground.

Trouble was aboard the first shuttle to ground. That wasn't SOP, but the guy who wrote the SOP book was writing for the average moron in command.

Trouble didn't consider himself a moron.

He also didn't consider himself prone to weeping, but he had to fight back tears.

Trouble had walked this street before, not a month ago. Then the dirt road had been lined with huts. Mothers sat in the shade, husking rice. Kids ran in the endless games they played, those that weren't old enough to care for the new crop of babies or help mom. In the fields beyond, men and women, old and young had planted a crop here or harvested a field there.

All Trouble saw were bodies today.

Old bodies. Young bodies. Large bodies. Small bodies. Tiny bodies.

Some had died from gunshot wounds. Others had been, what was the old saying, put to the sword.

It looked like a few had fought. He'd seen men and

woman in his last visit practicing their martial arts. He forgot the name they used for it, Ty Won Ko, or something. Beside a few bodies there was blood. Too much blood for one human.

Apparently, whoever had done this had taken their dead with them. Or maybe they'd buried them here. He'd have to order a search.

He'd have to wait until he got control of his voice before he ordered that search.

"God, General, who could have done this?" a young sergeant asked.

Trouble paused to see if God would answer. He certainly had none.

It was an hour before the searchers turned up a couple of kids. They'd been messing around in what passed for woods on this planet. They saw it all.

Of the four, only one was in any shape to share what they'd seen.

"They were big," she stammered.

"Big. Four eyes. Four of them," he said, using four fingers to point at his own pair.

"And a beak," another boy managed to add.

"Four legs. Four arms," the other one went on. "Some had things like guns. Most had these long sharp metal things. They'd go right . . ." and the rest was lost to a shriek of mourning.

Trouble ordered troops of the second wave to begin collecting the bodies.

"General Longknife, I think most of these folks were Buddhist," Trouble said, calling up to the ship. "I got lots of different stuff among my Savannah troops, but no Buddhists. There's a whole lot of people down here needing to be buried and I don't know exactly how to do it."

"We'll check among the cruisers," Ray Longknife answered. "There's bound to be some among their crews. Wardhaven has a thriving Buddhist community. At least I see them in the streets every lunar New Year."

"I see lots of Irish in the street on St. Patrick's Day. More in the pubs. I don't know what many of them are the other 364 days of the year," Trouble said, but left it to the bigger elephant.

Hard to think I'm an elephant here, now.

The search turned up no more living humans and no sign of those who had done this. With the situation well in hand, Trouble took the next longboat back up to the *Astute*.

"Is it as bad as it looks?" Ray Longknife asked as Trouble met with him, Rita, Becky and Crossie in the commodore's day quarters.

"It's worse. Down there, you can smell it. I got my crew wearing gas masks so they can breathe. And the bugs. I don't know where that planet got so many bugs that love to chow down on human corruption."

Rita and Becky looked to be turning green. Crossie was past green into white. He bolted for the head where the rest of them listened to him be explosively sick.

"That man needs to get out more," Trouble said. "See what this is really all about."

"Yeah," Rita said. "We've sent all this back in a coded message to Savannah, with secondary addresses to the Command staff on Wardhaven, Pitts Hope, New Eden, and anyplace else that was thinking of loaning us a ship."

"Earth, too," came from the head, but was followed by more sounds of breakfast explosively exiting.

"So, if I may ask," said Trouble, "what do we do now?"

"Gather our forces," Ray said. "Rita, have you got

anything back from the team you sent aboard the space station?"

"It's shot up too bad to use. Whoever attacked the planet made Swiss cheese of the station. The central computer is shot to hell, but we did find some stuff in archives that we could read."

She paused. Crossie, green as cheese himself, came to the door of the head to listen better.

"This is where Whitebred took his pirates. Somewhere along the line, the pirates got tired of his management style and offed him. They also split up. There's another pirate hideout named Port Elgin out past that jump we saw the aliens taking."

"Oh, shit," Trouble said. "More dead bodies?"

"That remains to be seen. There's also the mention of some Planet of Gold that the Big Fellows have."

"Big Fellows?" Becky echoed.

"The one kid we found that was coherent," Trouble said, "was sure the people who did this were ten feet tall and had four eyes, four arms and four legs. That sound familiar?"

"Oh, shit," Crossie said, wiping his mouth.

"So," Rita said, "we bury our dead. We wait for the rest of the ships to join us. Say in three, maybe five days. I've ordered comm to send the ships that were out on patrol to this planet's coordinates. If they can jump here without going through Savannah, it will save time."

"So we wait." Trouble said.

"And then we go see." Ray said.

34

Commodore Rita Nuu-Longknife put her crew through their paces. Drill, drill and more drill. They responded with grim determination.

They'd seen the pictures from LeMonte. The bodies shot had been bad. The bodies slit open, neck to groin were worse. The babies split through were unspeakable.

Maybe Rita should have censored the pictures.

But there was no way she could have kept the returning ground troops from spreading The Word among the stay-behind Sailors.

"How are we going to talk to the likes of the people that did this?" she shared with Becky Graven. The ambassador was the one person on board that she expected she could share her concerns with keeping this from getting out of hand and get a decent hearing.

Becky shook her head. "How *do* we talk to people who did that?" the diplomat answered.

"We've *got* to make peace?" Rita said.

"Yes, we have to, but on what terms? The only way they

could have made this worse was to have roasted the humans on an open fire and eaten them."

"Thank God they didn't." Rita said. She hadn't thought of that.

"I don't know what we're dealing with," the diplomat said. "I've been trained all my life to try to smooth over rough spots. Keep the peace. Find the middle ground. Where's the middle ground with that?"

"Do you have any idea what our pirates did to them?" Rita asked.

"I heard about this Planet of Gold," Becky said. "I haven't heard anything about us going there?"

"There isn't much in the database," Rita admitted. "I think we'll end up there."

"If you say so."

Now, four days after the discovery of the slaughter, Rita's squadron was closing on the jump into deeper space. Joining up with her was the second squadron. When they jumped in, Rita had ordered them to meet her at the jump out, and then sent them the report of what they'd found on LeMonte

The second squadron had gone to full drill and double watches.

Now the squadrons hung before the jump. Rita had the four Astutes, the *Patton*, and five Rambles formed up on her. The captains from the Wardhaven cruisers *Exeter*, *Northampton* and *Concord* had already signaled her that they would conform to her orders. The other divisions, the *Lion* and *Puma* from Lorna Do and the *Vampire* and *Fury* from Pitt's Hope might have questioned her right to command, but not a word had been raised. They fell in right behind her cruiser divisions. Nine transports came up the rear with troops and support elements for landing a reinforced division, or five regiments that could have formed a short corps if the last two regiments got time to get in some field exercises with the other three.

Rita sent a jump buoy through first. When it returned undamaged, she ordered the *Northampton* through and quickly followed with the *Astute* and her sisters.

The system was empty, though Matt reported that the sniffer found plenty of residual reaction mass with a significantly high sodium content. The trail led to the jump the information from LeMonte said would take them to Port Elgin.

Three jumps and three empty systems later, they did a very cautious approach to the jump that should take them to Port Elgin.

They jumped.

The system was empty.

The planet fourth from the system's star was quiet. Deathly quiet.

35

T rouble swore.

He'd sworn that he never wanted to see the likes of LeMonte again.

Now he swore as he walked another dusty street of slaughter.

It was as if he was living the nightmare all over again.

He tapped his commlink. "Ray, Rita, Becky. All of you. You've got to see this this time. You've got to smell it. Live it," he spat.

"We'll come down," Major General Ray Longknife answered him, "but you got to give us some time, Trouble. We think we've found the wreckage of a space battle."

"How bad of a battle?" Trouble asked, letting the distraction of murder above take his mind off of the murder below.

"Pretty bad," Ray said. "Rita says most of the ships blew when their reactors lost containment, though there is some wreckage, more than she expected. At least some of it looks alien."

"I'm glad to hear we got some of the bastards," Trouble said.

"If we can trust the initial reads, it isn't a lot."

"Damn," Trouble muttered.

"Have you found any survivors?" Ray asked.

"We're looking for them, but you have to understand, these bodies have been dead for a lot longer. A couple of weeks. Maybe a month. Hard to tell, what with all these alien animals and stuff nibbling on the bodies."

"I hear you. Pity any survivor who had to keep them company while they rotted."

"My thoughts entirely. Listen, you can send me down the Buddhists who did the rites for the dead on LeMonte? I'm not burning a single funeral pyre until you see what I'm looking at."

"We understand you, Trouble. I'll talk to Rita. See if she can delegate the search for a while."

"You think that will work? I don't win a lot of arguments with Ruth."

"If I tell her that I and Becky are going down, she'll come with us. I don't think she trusts me with Becky."

"I wouldn't trust any male with Becky," Trouble said. Ruth had had a talk with him about being alone on a ship with the lovely ambassador. He'd pointed out that he'd be sharing the ship with a whole lot of men and women.

"You know what I mean," his very pregnant wife had said.

"I know," he said, not knowing anything at all, except that he'd better agree with her at the moment.

Three hours later, Trouble was at the water's edge as the captain's gig from the *Astute* beached itself.

"What's that smell?" was Becky's first question as she waded ashore in a green ship's suit and army boots.

"The dead," Trouble said.

"Oh."

"Let's make this quick," Rita said. "I got a lost battle to examine and a battle of my own to plan."

"We leaving here?" Trouble said.

"As soon as we can," Ray said. "We're going looking for that Planet of Gold."

"I may have something for you," Trouble said, and produced a wrist unit. "Most of those we should have found are gone, but this one was hidden in a burned-out bungalow. Our tech squad has gone over it. It belonged to the guy running this show, at least the one left behind. He has a lot of recordings of meetings, including the one where they went chasing off, howling for gold."

"It mention anyone by the name of Black Bart?" Rita asked.

"Why?"

"We finally got a report from Savannah about that ship that tried to race in and out of the system cause 'the aliens were coming'. It belonged to a pirate of the name of Black Bart. We think he discovered and raided two alien planets besides the Planet of Gold."

"Shit," Trouble said. "If they did there what the aliens did here . . .?" didn't bear thinking about.

"That's kind of what I'm thinking," Rita said. "Pass what you've got up to Crossie. He's working with the scientific brain trust we have on the *Exeter* and *Northampton* to see what they can make of it."

They walked down the main street. It was a slow progress.

The visiting elephants had to pause to throw up. Even General Ray Longknife found the scene too much to take.

"We never did anything like this in the war. Not the Unity War. Not the planetary squabbling before Unity took over. This is inhuman," the general muttered, half to himself, half to persuade himself.

"I was kind of thinking that," Trouble said, "and don't feel bad about the stomach problem. I had mine already, back on LeMonte."

"I've seen enough," Rita said. "Becky?"

"It's going to be hard finding a peace after the likes of this. It's going to be hard finding a path to peace with the kind of animals that can do this," the diplomat said, her words hardened steel, and sharp to boot.

Rita nodded. "Trouble, you may deploy your burial details. You have no more than twenty-four hours. I'm taking the fleet out of orbit then. I want to get on the trail of the people who did this before it gets any colder."

"Aye, aye, ma'am," and Trouble turned to do the last thing he could do for these people.

36

Rita came awake. She fought the urge to claw her way into Ray's chest.

The waking nightmare of decaying ghosts demanding she remember them had her chest pounding and sweat pouring off of her.

With an effort, she slowed her breathing and forced the hammering of her heart to quiet.

"You awake?" Ray said beside her.

"Something like that."

"Was the nightmare bad?"

"How have you lived with them? If I'd known, I would have been . . ." Rita ran out of words. What could anyone do for someone to make this sort of thing better?

"My wars were bad, but not like this," Ray said, rolling over to face her. His fingers made circles around her breasts, then narrowed the circle to end up nipping at her hardening nipples.

"Please don't," she said. "The dead are too close at the moment."

"Sometimes the only way you can drive away the dead is to celebrate life."

"I don't feel much like celebrating."

"I know what you mean," Ray said, but he didn't roll away from her.

"Was this what you were going through when I, ah, did what I did?"

"When you damn near raped me to get pregnant with little Alex?" had a grin attached to it.

"I guess I did rather refuse to let you wallow in your self-pity. But this isn't self-pity."

"Isn't it? Isn't it all about you?"

"I thought it was about them."

"*They're* dead, love. We've said prayers at their pyres. All we can do for them, we've done. The rest *is* about us."

"So, what do we do?"

"We get on with our lives. We do what we have to do."

"And what, General Longknife, would you say that is?"

"A lot of things," his hands were back, circling her breasts. "We celebrate that we're not dead yet. And we tell those bastards that they do not treat humans like that."

"Well," Rita said, "let's celebrate being not dead yet. Then we'll go talk to the bastards."

And they were not even late for breakfast.

Crossie was there, with some boffins borrowed from the *Northampton*. Included was a slip of a gal with the soft and sharp-clawed moniker of Kat.

"We're sure we know where the Planet of Gold is," Kat said while Crossie was taking a deep breath to start what would be a long lecture carefully nuanced and with many caveats.

"How many jumps?" Rita asked.

"Five."

"Any idea how many human ships were destroyed here? Or alien ships?" Rita shot back, rapid fire.

"Eight to ten humans," Kat said. "Maybe two aliens."

"That lopsided," Ray said.

"It looks that way," Crossie got in fast. "I have no explanation why we did so poorly."

"Maybe the pirates didn't drill so much or maintain their lasers very well," Kat snuck in.

"I tend to agree with you, Kat," Rita said. She paused for only a moment, then went on. "Is there any reason for us not to head out?"

From the next table over, Trouble put in his two cents. "We've finished burying the dead. I'm ready to make some of them four eyed bastards ready for the undertaker's fine trade."

"Then let's get this fleet underway."

Four jumps later, the squadron was at a halt before the jump that would likely bring them to the Planet of Gold.

"There's been traffic here," Matt reported from the *Northampton*. "Sniffer finds plenty of reaction mass left behind. More salt than there should be."

"May I have the honor of leading the jump?" Captain Izzy Umboto of the *Patton* requested.

"Please do."

The *Patton* drifted up to the jump, then nudged itself through.

Rita had the *Astute* right behind her. "Put us through," she ordered the jump master.

The stars wavered, and then came back different.

"There's a planet third from this sun," Sensors reported. "And I make out a whole lot of reactors in orbit around it.

None of the reactors conform to anything we've built in human space."

Rita grinned. "So, bastards. Will you run or will you fight?"

37

The answer to Rita's question hung in the balance for a long hour as her fleet followed her through the jump, then formed on her *Astute* as she set a fleet acceleration of one gee toward the third planet.

Each report from Sensors was the same. "They remain in orbit, ma'am. Reactors are active, but no reaction to our presence.

As the second hour flowed into the third, Rita decided that their intention was to wait for her in orbit.

Or maybe strike out at her as she came into orbit.

"We'll be braking," she muttered to Ray as he stood beside her command chair. "They'll have a shot up our vulnerable fantail at our jets and reactors."

"That sounds bad."

"That is bad. That's what the humans had at Port Elgin. So how come it didn't work all that well for them there?"

Ray raised an eyebrow at the question.

"That really was a question, General. I'd really like to know."

"Well, it didn't work for the pirates there. I'm sure that

my brilliant commodore can figure out how to make it not work for these bastards this time, either."

"I love your confidence in me," Rita said, dryly.

Still, Ray had a point. The supposed advantage of a defender had not worked out all that well for the pirates. Had it just been poor maintenance and ship handling? How good were the people, aliens, whatever, facing her? How battle-tested was their commander?

Rita, who'd seen a lot of how it shouldn't be done in the Unity War, now had a chance to show them how it should be done.

She left the bridge under her XO's able command and retired to her in-space cabin. Ray joined her. She left him the chair, and settled herself on the bunk, staring up at the overhead.

Why can't engineers get us a high gee seat that's as comfortable as a bunk?

"I'm incoming. Backing my way into orbit," she muttered to herself. "They can gauge pretty much when I'll get there and adjust themselves in their orbit so they can come charging out at me, aiming for my stern.

She paused to picture this in her mind's eye.

"I can flip ship and fire my forward batteries, present them with the thickest armor of my dust catcher." Rita played that out in her mind's eye.

"I might miss making orbit, or have to do some real honking around to make it."

"But if they launch out at you," Ray put in, "won't that mean that you get to make orbit while they're headed off for who knows where?"

"Good point, my ground-pounding friend," Rita said and tapped her commlink. "Sensors, how much activity can you make out on the planet?"

"There are shuttles going up and down. The pace seems to be constant. It hasn't picked up. We're getting communications off the planet. Nothing we can read, though. There are no reactors on the ground. It looks to be pretty primitive down there."

"XO, Sensors, let me know the second anything changes?"

"We will," came back immediately.

Rita continued to stare at the overhead, seeing lines of battle swinging in, up, down and around the planet's gravity well.

Once she had an idea of what she wanted, she called the Jump Master, the best navigator aboard and laid out a plan.

A half hour later, the monitor above the desk of her in-space cabin came to life. Ray swapped places with her, taking the bed but looking over her shoulder. On the screen, dots danced through one iteration after another.

Rita studied one result after another, then went through the whole thing again . . . differently. Finally, she reran a few with different variations.

She and Ray swapped places again, and she eyed the overhead, letting her mind wander through various lines of thought. She got up, and, without moving Ray, added another question to her last list, then slipped back into the bunk.

This went on for two hours, with Ray keeping quiet vigil. That was mighty nice of him. She spent another long session at the work station, came to like what she saw, then took Ray to supper in the wardroom.

He did a good job of making her laugh. The watching officers seemed to find that encouraging, their skipper laughing at her husband's jokes. Trouble added his own two cents' worth, and Becky, no real surprise, turned out to have a decidedly wicked collection of dirty jokes.

Dinner over, Rita checked in on the bridge. The enemy was still not changing their position. In a way, that bothered Rita.

Someone clearly thought they didn't need to turn in any cards. The hand they held was pat.

All Rita could do was hope they were wrong.

Rita invited Ray back to her in-space cabin and walked him through her thoughts. She didn't really expect a gravel-cruncher to be an expert in three dimensional vectors around a gravity well, but he listened intently, asking a few rather good questions. And then suggested they make a night of it.

"Thanks for the offer, trooper, but momma's gonna sleep right here, off the bridge," she told her husband.

"You don't trust them to not change things up in the night?"

"Not one bit. They haven't changed anything. That doesn't mean they won't."

"Sweet dreams, love. Don't let the bed bugs bite," he said, and kissed her on the forehead.

"They wouldn't dare," she said, and smiled him out the door.

Then she lay down, flat on her back, stared at the over-head and let the vectors run.

A blessing that night, the vectors kept the ghosts at bay.

38

The navigator who had the morning watch sent a runner to wake Rita at 0500. "Ma'am, the XO says they are making their move," the young man said, standing in the doorway.

Rita quickly splashed water on her face, and went to see what that move was.

"They started juggling themselves in orbit about ten minutes ago," said the XO as she surrendered the conn when Rita came on the bridge.

"We've been getting an improved picture of them, skipper," reported the lieutenant on Sensors.

"Talk to me."

"There are three of them that we've taken to calling quads, ma'am, though Nav here thinks we should call them four deckers," the XO said through a grin.

"I always said you read too many books about Napoleonic era sailing ships," Rita said.

The gal on Nav just grinned back, unrepentantly.

"All the ships we're facing are ball-shaped," Sensors continued. "The quads have four reactors spaced at ninety degrees around the sphere. They have capacitors, or something that stores energy forward of the reactors. Likely, they have lasers forward of that."

"That would match the one report we have," Nav said.

"I agree," Rita said.

"They have six of what we are calling triples, or triple deckers."

"Leave the 'decker' off," Rita snapped. "The second we save may save our life, lieutenant."

"Yes, Commodore," Sensors said, and then went on. "They have three reactors spaced at 120 degrees around the sphere. The capacitors or whatever are about half as powerful as those on the quads."

"That's a major drop down," Nav observed.

"That would appear so," Rita said, rubbing her chin in thought.

"The rest of the twenty ships are doubles, ma'am. They have two reactors spaced evenly at 180 degrees from each other. The capacitors are about half as strong as the triples."

"What kind of density are those ships showing us?" Rita asked.

"The quads are giving the atom laser a good wiggle, ma'am. There's some serious mass there. The other two types seem rather hollow. Much less dense."

"Less dense," Nav said. "Less powerful power storage units."

"So why are there so many?" Rita asked herself. She had brought eleven heavy cruisers to this shindig. She had six light cruisers and nine transports. Eight of the transports were hovering at the jump point, with orders to run if things went bad. The last one was back on the other side of the jump keeping a check on their line of retreat.

The hostiles' deployment did not make a lot of sense,

unless someone had come with only what they had available.

Clearly, it had been enough to shoot up a pirate fleet.

Pirates are one thing. This time you drew the Navy, you murdering bastards.

Of course, the present Navy was only what Rita had been able to beg, borrow, and steal. The crews and commanders were what could be found sober, or eager, and the whole collection was under the command of a jumped-up transport pilot.

Stow that in whatever hole it crawled out of, she ordered herself.

"In the last fifteen minutes," Nav said, checking the watch on the bottom of the main screen, "they have started juggling their order in orbit. When you went to get some sleep, they were strung out pretty equally in orbit, kind of like a bunch of pearls on a string. Now they're changing that line-up. Some ships are going into high orbits, some dropping lower. It will take a while for them to settle down."

"Thank you for waking me," Rita said. It was a good thing when a watch officer isn't afraid to ruin the skipper's sleep.

Rita looked down at yesterday's rumpled uniform. She didn't have to check to know she was distinctly smelly. It was one thing for her husband to come back from a hard day in the field smelling like he'd had a skunk for lunch. It was something different entirely for a ship's skipper to have an aroma.

"I'll be in my quarters, getting a shower and a change of clothes. If anything changes drastically, don't hesitate to have a female runner drag me out of the shower."

"Yes, ma'am. Sorry about sending a male runner," Nav

said. "The female runner had left earlier to chase down some fresh coffee. Would you like some?"

"I don't mind a guy waking me. Getting me out of the shower? That's different."

"We could send a guy and have him encourage your husband to get you out of the shower," Sensors whispered.

Rita made an effort not to hear that as she left.

In her quarters, Ray was sleeping, she tiptoed past him and shot through a quick shower. Ray was up when she got out; a new blue shipsuit was laid across their bed.

"Thanks," she said pulling on a bra. "Could you drop down to the galley and get me a plate of fresh bread and butter? Maybe some hot coffee? They just got a new pot on the bridge, but I suspect it will be cold by now."

"Yes, Commodore," Ray said, "the major general hears and will obey."

"Well, my Army major general," Rita answered in full sassy mode, "whether you're alive or dead tonight will depend on how your Navy commodore does today."

"Then I better get her caffeine level up and some nice bread in her belly before she starts taking heads off that don't have four eyes."

He gave her a peck on the cheek and was gone.

Rita ran a quick comb through the short mop that passed for her hair at the moment and returned to the bridge. She'd been gone fifteen minutes.

Nothing had changed where the enemy was concerned.

On the bridge, everyone was now in a high gee station. The chief of the boat brought one onto the bridge and parked it beside Rita's command chair. She slipped into it and he hit the toggle switches that freed her chair from its lock-downs.

Quickly he rolled it off the bridge as she motored her station around and slid her board over it.

She was ready; now where was the enemy? No, hostiles. She didn't want to start thinking of the aliens as enemies just yet.

There ought to be some formal declaration of war or something.

Admittedly that might be hard with them not even knowing each other's languages or being able to patch into each other's comm lines.

With the enemy reorganizing, it was time to reorganize her own forces.

"Squadron, form a box on me," she ordered and the *Astute* slowed its deceleration to let her three trailing sisters form up on her, each 300 kilometers from the other.

"*Lion*, please form a square of your squadron, 500 kilometers aft of mine and 500 kilometers to starboard. Set a 300-klick interval between ships and prepare to jink ship on my command."

"Aye, aye, commodore," came back from the senior Lorna Do skipper, and the four ships from there and Pitts Hope moved into Rita's desired fighting array.

"*Northampton*, form the second Wardhaven squadron on my port side, same intervals."

"Aye, aye," Matt responded. He had battle time in cruisers, but the former merchant skipper had told Rita he had no desire to carry the full burden of command. Now he obeyed as she sent them all into battle.

"*Patton*, form the light cruisers into two divisions on our wings. Use the same intervals."

"Aye, aye, Commodore," Izzy responded. She had more time in the Navy than any officer in the fleet. More time than most of the chiefs. However, all but the last few years of it had been served in the Navy's ground-based defense battalions. Rita had more ship time than Izzy.

Today, she'd cover the wings and be ready, with her two pint-size squadrons to move to clean up what crumbs Rita's heavies left to flee.

Assuming this fight goes anywhere close to what I have planned.

This array put the super heavies in the lead. Their 9.2-inch lasers had the longest range. The ice armor swathing the hull was a meter and a half thick. The trailing heavy cruisers sported 8-inch lasers for their main battery, and ice a meter and a quarter. The *Patton* had 6-inch lasers and a meter of armor. Sadly, the Rambling scout cruisers' armor was a thin half meter despite their 6-inch main battery. They'd been lightened up for extra range to do their exploration mission.

Today they'd fight. A mission that had always been considered secondary.

Life doesn't let you just do what you want, the co-Minister for Exploration sighed.

We came out here looking, and look what we found.

She let a sigh escape her, but her eyes were on the fleet. It was forming up according to her orders.

Time would tell if she'd done it better than the admirals she'd bitched about following in the war. Admirals who'd lost their battles, and with it, the lives of so many of Rita's friends.

"May they be truly grateful for what they are about to receive," Rita's XO half-prayed at her elbow.

"Amen," Rita answered.

39

The alien fleet came out from behind the Planet of Gold in their battle array. In many ways, it mimicked Rita's.

The three quads were in a triangle formation in the lead. The triangle was pointed up, course straight for Rita's fleet. Trailing them were the six triples in two triangles as well, one on each flank, though these triangles were pointed down. Stretching out on their flank were two squares of four doubles.

"No, one is a box. The other is a triangle," Hesper, on sensors, corrected her report.

"Where are the rest?" Rita asked.

"Ah, oh. There they are," Hesper said, a few seconds later. "Three of the doubles are out ahead of the quads, ma'am. They're in a very irregular triangle."

"That's a strange deployment," the XO observed. "And a simple one. They're going to charge at each other and shoot as we pass. Not all that much thought behind it."

"Maybe enough," Rita said. "Come to think of it, the wreckage off Port Elgin fits this kind of mad charge."

"Yes," the XO agreed.

"We're missing a ship," Rita pointed out.

"I'm hunting for it," Hesper replied. "I think I've got it. Yes, there's a ship hightailing it for the Gamma Jump out of here."

"Someone doesn't want to fight," the XO said.

"Or someone has orders to run for reinforcements or to let someone know what's happening here," Rita said. The data allowed for many interpretations.

Few of them were very good for her fleet.

Rita leaned forward in her high gee station. She'd gone to two gees to slow herself down a bit sooner, give herself some leeway to flip ship on the final approach. At two gees, she really wasn't relying on the station for much support. Later, if she went for a burst at the max, three gees, she'd need it dearly if she didn't want to black out.

"Why are those three small doubles out in front?" she muttered, half to herself.

"To draw our fire? To see what we have?" XO offered. "Maybe they have rockets they want to get off at us?"

"Maybe their sensor package has a short range and those are trying to get a better handle on us," Sensor suggested.

"We'll see," Rita whispered, still deep in thought. The scattered light ships did not make any sense, unless they were a sacrificial gambit.

And why start with a sacrificial ploy?

Then she got her first surprise of the day.

"Skipper," Hesper reported from Sensors, "the three lead ships are deploying junk. Sparklers, radar decoys, heat sources. All kind of junk as well as ice and sand, if I'm making it right."

"Why do that?" the XO muttered before Rita did herself.

Then it got more interesting.

"Ma'am, the three quads are sliding off to our right."

Which left Rita frowning. She'd intended to edge to the left, go for a high orbit and keep her vulnerable engines aimed a bit off from the approaching fleet.

Now, if she did that, she'd be opening the range from the enemy's main force.

"You sure of that course change?" she asked of Sensors.

"Mostly, ma'am," Hesper reported. "Radar, mass analysis, lasers, all of them are reporting the change. Visuals is having a problem following them through all this gunk, though."

"A problem?" Rita asked.

"Those three leading doubles, ma'am, the stuff they're scattering is chaff, sparklers, and heaters. It makes it hard to see what's behind them."

"Why would they do that?" the XO murmured.

"Hesper, you remember the last time someone put a lot of gunk up ahead of our intrepid Navy? We damn near lost our fleet to those Society Slugs," Rita muttered, remembering a landing on one minor satellite that did not go at all as planned.

"All too well, ma'am. I'm doing my best to see through that gunk, but I'm not having a lot of luck."

"Maybe we should make some luck," Rita said.

There was nothing here that made much sense. *But these are aliens I'm fighting, right? They're not like us.*

"Guns," Rita called. "Have Turret X target the nearest quad."

"We're not even at extreme range, yet," he said, but two 9.2-inch lasers reached out.

And hit nothing.

"Those should have been right on," Guns snapped,

offended by the miss. "Not good for much more than lighting them up, but we should have hit them."

"Guns, target all aft 5-inch secondaries for the space between the two triangles of triples. Paint the area."

"Painting, skipper, but that's all they'll do."

Six 5-inch lasers reached out to crisscross the vacant space where the quads had been. They burned chaff, sparklers, and heaters that the lead alien scouts had scattered.

And lit up three large balls of death that were not at all where the sensors placed them.

"Hell, what are they doing there?" Sensors growled.

"Squadron, target quads with aft main batteries. Fire," Rita ordered, then added. "Squadron, begin jinking. Put on battle revolutions."

The lights dimmed as all available power was shunted to reloading the emptying aft capacitors. The *Astute* dropped under Rita, throwing her against the harness of her high gee station, then rose, slamming her butt against the water cushions.

A worse affront to her inner ear was the spin the ship took on. Twenty revolutions a minute slammed Rita against the back of her seat.

Doing a jig might throw off the hostiles' aim because not getting hit was best. Ice armor was there to absorb lasers when you couldn't dodge them. But even ice could take only so much heat.

Spinning a ship assured that even a laser's power would not burn through the ice before the spin swung the void of vaporized ice away and layered more ice in place.

Then Rita was thrown right, left, left some more, with a drop thrown in that made her stomach ride up in her throat.

They were dodging and spinning, but the hostiles weren't shooting.

Yet.

"Flip ships," Rita ordered, and the *Astute* spun around to present her nose to the onrushing hostiles.

"Fire forward batteries."

On screen, the external visuals caught the hint of light as invisible 9.2-inch lasers cut through the scattered gunk to hammer into the three alien balls. Two of them looked to be hit bad.

Then all three of them reached out with sixteen lasers that shone as they too, made gunk burn. And every one of them pinned the *Alacrity* for a horrible moment.

Steam spun off into space as ice and spin struggled to do more than it should have been asked of them.

A turret popped up to fire as the spin took it right into the burn of an enemy laser.

The turret exploded.

Then the *Alacrity* was spinning off its tortured ice, and lasers were cutting right through her. She burned, then glowed, and suddenly was no more.

"Flip ships," Rita ordered. "Angle 25 degrees away from the base course." That should protect their engines . . . some.

"Fire," Rita ordered. Maybe she shouted.

"We are in range," the *Lion* reported.

"*Lion*, engage quads. *Northampton*, engage the closest doubles.

All three of the quads were hurting, falling off course as first one, then another of their reactors took hits and angle of forces failed to balance. This time, their fire was sporadic as they cut loose with one or two lasers from only a few of their pods.

One exploded, its reactors eating the ship as their thermonuclear heated plasma got loose.

The leading doubles seemed to evaporate like water on a hot griddle as *Exeter*, *Northampton*, and *Concord* took them under fire.

But now the triples were coming into the fight. Their three pods sprouted two lasers each.

Someone must have commanded there because all six reached out for Rita's squadron. Two lasers raked the *Astute*. They failed to achieve ice break through, but the *Astute* throbbed as the evaporated ice threw the balance of her spin off.

But the *Astute* was a good ship. Pumps hummed as reaction mass was thrust from one tank to another to keep the ship balanced.

Dan Taussig's *Artful* was not so lucky. Maybe she took more hits. Maybe some new machinery failed to meet its warranty. Whatever it was, she spun out of control for only a moment, but the pause in her jig was enough for more lasers to slash into her. A turret exploded.

"*Artful*, pull away," Rita ordered.

"Going to three gees deceleration," Dan shouted, and the *Artful* tried to let the rest of the squadron pass her. She tried, but the engines failed him and he stayed, pinned by more lasers.

"Helm, put us between the *Artful* and the skunks," Rita ordered.

"Adjusting jinking pattern," helm reported.

"Flip ships," Rita ordered. The fleet flipped. The reloaded batteries from ten human cruisers reached out for the hostile six triples.

They had begun a slow dodge and weave, nothing like

the human jinking pattern. They did not spin, which led Rita to suspect they had no armor.

Under the fire of sixty lasers, they burned.

Two blew up. Three began to come apart like rose petals in a child's curious hand.

Children can be so unconscious in their violence.

The murder at Rita's shouted orders was done with pure intent.

Some of the doubles tried to run, to break off, to fight the physics of their fate.

They ran into the concerted fire of the entire human fleet as the scout cruiser's 6-inch lasers came in range.

What whizzed by the human fleet as they passed the aliens was wrack and ruin.

Rita hardly noticed, she was busy taking the measure of her own fleet and the damage it had taken in just a few short, gut-wrenching minutes.

One big cruiser lost, one damaged, was only the start of the accounting.

40

R ita breathed a short prayer of thanksgiving, then turned her full attention to the butcher bill. "Nori, is your *Arduous* in any shape to help Dan?"

"They hit us a few glancing blows. I'll stand by the *Artful* and render all assistance possible."

"Dan, you take the *Artful* into any orbit you can manage."

"I've still got power, but we've got some internal fires we're working on. I've vented as many compartments to space as I can. Some of the automatic doors aren't as automatic as they used to be."

"Take care," Rita said, and then moved on to her other problems.

"XO, what's our state?"

"Reactors ready to answer all bells. We've been holed at frames 172 through 179, radii a and b. Nothing we can't handle. I've got teams out repairing armor."

"Nav, can we make a good orbit?"

"The first orbit will be a bit rough, but we can regularize it by the third go around."

"Make it so," Rita ordered.

Her duty to her squadron and ship done, she turned her attention to the fleet. There had been a few hits from the doubles on the other cruisers, but nothing that had defeated the heavy's armor. The Rambling Rose had taken a hit to its rocket motor but was making for orbit with what she had left.

"Undamaged light cruisers, set an orbit that will bring you back through the wreckage of the alien battle group," Rita ordered. "Check for survivors."

"We'll do that, Commodore," Izzy replied on net, "but I didn't see anything that looked like survival pods as we went by. We're also not making out any distress signals. Not a one, ma'am."

"They can't be that stupid," Rita said.

"How many survival pods did we make out among the wreckage where the pirates fought them?" Izzy asked.

"But there must have been survival pods."

"They bought used warships," Izzy said. "They were sure to keep the guns but survival pods have their own surplus market. I don't think the pirates bothered to buy them."

"And neither did these dolts," Rita said.

"You thinking what I'm thinking?" Izzy said.

"That our pirates fell afoul of their pirates, or something enough the same as to make no-never-mind?"

"That's my first guess," Izzy said. "But I'm open to being proved wrong."

"Those three quads didn't fight like pirates," Rita pointed out. "They messed good with our sensors, too. The others didn't, I think."

"Yeah, that kind of bothers me," Izzy said.

"Well, let's clean up whatever of this mess we can and see what happens next."

"Do you want to order in the transport fleet?" Izzy asked.

That brought a frown to Rita's lips. "I don't like the look of that one that maybe ran, or maybe was running for help. Let's see if the troops on the heavy cruisers are enough to get us a decent recon of the Planet of Gold. If you don't think you'll need two of the scouts for policing up this battlefield, send them off to provide some cover for the transports but keep them holding at the jump point."

"Those green troopers are gonna love spending their time in zero gee."

"They joined the army. They got to expect shitty orders," the Navy commodore said, with a sly grin.

"You busy?" Ray asked from behind her.

"Just cleaning up loose ends. Speaking of, you need to put together a landing party to check out the Planet of Gold."

"Should I issue gold panning equipment?"

"I don't think they'll have time," Rita said. "We may have company coming, but I want to know what happened down there. The one report we've got leaves a lot to be desired where specifics are concerned. I don't much care for the gloss some folks were putting on their carrying on down there. I want to have someone I trust take a look for themselves."

"And I know just the man for the mission," Ray said and tapped his commlink.

"Trouble, have I got a job for you."

Rita had no trouble catching the groan that followed her husband's cheery words.

41

B revet Brigadier General Trouble was getting tired of this shit. If he saw another dead and bloated body, he was going to puke.

Problem was, he hadn't felt the need to puke once on this drop.

That was starting to bother him.

"You getting used to this shit?" he muttered to himself, or were these alien bodies somehow not driving him to the need to puke.

There were a lot of bodies, all with too many arms, legs and empty eye sockets. Here, however, someone had stacked them up like cordwood. Had they intended to bury or burn them? That was possible. Rita and her fleet certainly had not been expected.

But there were other dead. They'd found a cemetery outside the hurriedly built wall around the town. Actually, they'd found several. One had crosses. One six pointed stars. Another had five pointed stars. The last just had markers over boxes of ashes. That one had been the largest.

A lot of humans had died here.

Trouble went down to the beach. General Ray Longknife was coming to take his own look at what Trouble had found. Trouble had sent plenty of pictures up to the *Astute*. It was nice working for an elephant that took the time to really check out the lay of the land.

Or of the dead.

To Trouble's surprise, Commodore Rita Nuu-Longknife followed the general ashore. And right behind her was Becky Graven, the ambassador. The weasel Crossie had actually come down with them.

All the elephants were on parade.

Major General Ray Longknife looked around. "Was there an assault here?" he asked.

"I think it was more of a fighting withdrawal," Trouble said. "We found wreckage washed up along the beach of at least one shuttle. Humans bodies had been collected in a heap over there, under the trees. There's some interesting patches where lasers turned the sand to glass. From the bones caught up in the glass, I'd guess there were a lot of aliens down on the beach. Final protective fire is my guess."

Ray nodded agreement.

"What else have you got to show us?"

Trouble began the grand tour.

"Wall and ditch here were hastily dug," he said, ushering them through the gate. "There are sandbagged positions on the top of the wall, but nothing down here."

"Have you had any reactions from the aliens?" Rita asked.

"They tossed a sack of incendiaries in here a bit after we arrived. We got up a radar so when they tossed the second round, we had mortar bombs backtracking them. There was no third round," Trouble said with a proud chuckle.

His troops were green. That didn't mean they were incompetent. They were rapidly taking on the patina of vets.

"This place has been burned out," the ambassador observed.

"Burned, rebuilt, burned and was being rebuilt again," Trouble said.

"Someone doesn't know when to quit," Rita said.

"A lot of people, I'd say," Trouble offered. "There's one place I need to show you."

They headed for the one significant structure inside the walls.

"Over there seemed to be a meeting hall. We found lots of human liquor bottles, jugs, and such. There was a wooden sign, ripped down and tossed aside saying CAPTAIN'S HOUSE."

"As in pirate captain's house." Becky said.

"I think somebody had read too many bad historical romance tales," Rita observed.

"This mess here and in space sure looks like it," Ray said.

"There's one room I think you'll find informative," Trouble said, and led them within.

"Before we shipped out, I snatched up some guys from Savannah's police forensic unit. They've gone over this particular room with some interest,"

Trouble held open a large wooden door. Its planks were reinforced with iron bands and it had a large, broken lock.

"The roof was burned off at least once by laser fire," he said, pointing at the ceiling with its fresh cut logs and thatch. "The gouges you see in the adobe walls were put there by molten gold splatter. Most had been dug out by the time we got here. There were still small droplets of gold that our team recovered."

"What's in the sacks there?" Becky asked.

"More gold nuggets. This is someone's, or several groups of competing peoples' treasure room. The boxes have silver bars from the mine up in the hill. We've flown a recon over it, and were shot at when we took our drone in low. We've left it alone. Oh, those smaller sacks have some really fantastic jewels in them. Diamonds, rubies, emeralds."

"No wonder you have four guards at that door," Ray said.

"And I change them every hour. They're not supposed to know what's in here, but I think the rumor's starting to spread."

"I'm tempted to slag this from orbit like someone already did," Rita said, "but I think we'd better take it back as evidence."

"Evidence of what?" Ray said.

"Evidence that a lot of what we've been looking at was done in the throes of gold fever," Becky said.

Rita nodded. "I was wondering how anyone could be so unhuman. Now I'm starting to see. We humans don't have a very good track record for milk of human kindness when we're in the grip of gold fever. I'm suspecting that whoever these other big dudes are, they might not be representative of their species. At least I'm hoping they aren't. Maybe, if we can find some of them that aren't in thrall to filthy lucre, we might be able to have a reasonable conversation."

"That may be our only hope," Becky said.

"I think you're letting hope become your policy," Ray said. "Until we've pounded some respect for humanity into their thick heads, I don't expect them to be much interested in anything from us but our dying gasp."

"I hadn't taken you for such a bloody pessimist," Rita said to her husband.

"I hadn't taken you for such a blind optimist," Ray said back.

"Folks, can we do our policy forming somewhere else?" Trouble asked. "Preferably with this place receding fast in the rear-view mirror."

"I'll second that motion," Becky said.

"Trouble," Major General Ray Longknife ordered, "have your troops get this 'evidence' moved up to the *Astute*. Commodore, as soon as your fleet is ready to answer bells, I suggest that we get out of here before any more of those things shows up."

"On that, General, we most certainly agree," the general's wife responded. "Humanity has to know what has happened here."

"And what may be following us back," Ray added.

"Pity them that tries," Trouble muttered, "they'll wish they'd never been born."

F ather Joseph lay face down on a gold-inlayed marble floor. It was cold, but at least he'd been allowed to dress for his presentation to the Emperor.

He had lain once before on a floor. It had been a simple wooden floor in front of the altar of the parish church. Then, he'd arisen a priest forever, in the order of Melchizedek.

Whether he rose from this prostration, or died where he lay, would be decided with no comment from him.

Roth'sum'We'sum'Quin of the Chap'sum'We clan had made it quite clear to Joseph. "Of our words, you hear some. Of our words, most would kill you for what comes from your mouth. You are most impious."

For the act of being impious among these people, death was the only accepted apology.

And these folks were really into apologies. The bloodier the better.

This meeting would determine who owed the Emperor an apology. Roth, for taking one of the newly discovered animals into the city of the Emperor, or someone else for something Joseph didn't quite understand.

He huddled prostrate on the floor and tried to make sense of the few words he understood.

He had come into the Magnificent Hall of Celestial Reception with Roth and several senior members of his clan. Roth himself was just a fledgling.

His elders hoped that his youth and curiosity might be used in his favor to balance out his present folly.

But that was not the only thing on the agenda, if Joseph understood how these creatures thought. There was something else. Something he struggled to catch.

Even after a year of Roth helping him to understand their language and he trying to give Roth some grasp of human Standard, there was still so much that went over Father Joseph's head.

It wasn't the words, but the ideas behind the words.

Impious for one. To Father Joseph, it had a clear meaning, and a clear area. Matters of faith and morals. To these people, it seemed to cover just about everything, from political to scientific and everything in between.

Joseph wondered if he was missing some fine point of nuance that separated one sort of impiety from another, but if there was one, it eluded him.

For now, he was the one accused of being impious.

The room was large, much larger than any room Father Joseph had ever seen on Santa Maria. The entire village of Hazel Dell could fit in here, with room for the sheep to graze around the edges.

Not that there was any grass growing on the gold veined marble floor and pillars that supported a roof almost too far above his head to see.

Not that Joseph had seen much.

When he'd been brought in, windrows of thin, gauzy curtains rich in gold thread had hidden the visage of the Emperor from view. During his exactly dozen kowtows between slowly walking forward, Joseph had been able to catch views of hundreds of vividly dressed courtiers. They went in for bright blues, yellows and a few were in the imperial red. All were heavily worked with silver and gold thread sprinkled with jewels of every color.

Joseph's clothes had been a plain white. White was the color of death. Roth had warned him of that. "You are already dead. It will only be a flick of the Emperor's wrist to make you real dead. Do you love your chosen one?"

"Yes, I love my grandson," Joseph had said, refusing to use the Iteeche word for adoption but holding tight to the human way of blood line.

Roth had snorted. "You scum eating bottom feeder; your stiff neck will be the death of you yet."

"My persistence is the strength of my people," Joseph said. It had taken him six months to discover those words.

"You are persistent, but will that help you swim to the surface?"

"I am alive and with you."

"Which raises the question to the surface of roiling waters, am I the empty-headed one?"

"You are the wise one who has asked questions where others have only closed their eyes. What will you swim into with closed eyes, even if you do swim to the surface?"

"Your tongue is too sharp, limpet. You have hitched yourself to me. Do you suck my blood?"

"I eat what the wise one puts before me," even if it is raw fish, Joseph did not say. Fresh raw fish was the food of the wise, strong and powerful. The poor naked peasants ate something like yams and seaweed.

Joseph had survived on that for long enough.

In the Celestial Hall a long singsong prayer for wisdom was concluding and talk was starting up again. It went fast, and Joseph caught less than one word in four. Still, the direction was clear.

Several of the courtiers wanted all the humans dead.

If Joseph failed, his grandson would die along with the rest of the passengers and crew from the *Prosperous Goose*.

The leader of Roth's clan spoke slowly when he answered the charge of impiety against the humans. Maybe it was to let Joseph follow. Maybe it was to make it easy for the Emperor to follow something that had never been brought before an Emperor in ten thousand years. That wasn't just a phrase, there really had been an Emperor for that long.

The Iteeche didn't go in for change.

It would not be easy to convince this court that killing a few strange animals would not change the fact that the two different space-faring peoples were about to be thrown together.

The debate rambled on with the delicacy of teen girls gathering wild flowers, and doing their best to attract the eye of one particular boy among the throng also, supposedly out to gather spring flowers.

How many times had Father Joseph stood witness at the wedding before the flowers wilted?

He searched for such happy memories to keep his heart from pounding out of his chest.

A bell rang soft and clear.

"Who seeks entrance to the Imperial Presence?" rang out from one of the guards beside the throne."

Joseph did not catch the name. Roth's elders sought to

keep this reception to themselves, to have this question answered, but admission was granted.

Apparently, he who sought admission was one who could not be kept out.

He must also have been powerful, the curtains were not drawn closed, and the official in red garments approached the throne with only six kowtows.

"Who is the scum-sucking bottom-feeder?" the new one demanded.

"A wayfaring sailor, oh wise and powerful master of the Golden Satrap," came from Roth's elder. The use of the language told Joseph just how powerful this one was.

"They are murderers, no better than masterless men. They should all be killed."

"Oh, wise leader of many men, master of many gold mines, you have knowledge of this miserable animal's kind," was slathered in butter. Even more butter than these Iteeche usually used.

"Maybe I have," had a lot less force behind it.

"Could it be that you have brought less gold and silver to market these last moons because some animals like these have caused you trouble?"

"No animal like these can cause me any trouble."

"Then maybe your wisdom and harmony would not be bothered if my chosen one kept this as a mere pet."

"They are too dangerous to make good pets, you silver-tongued eel."

"And what have they done to show you that side of their nature?"

There was a rustle of fine cloth as the one in red turned ostentatiously to the throne. "These masterless scum-eaters have destroyed three imperial ships. That is how I know the poison in the fangs of these bottom feeders. I ask the mercy of the throne to call out the ships of my satrap. To crew them and arm them and send them forth to battle these rodents of filthy habits."

Breath left Joseph. It was no longer a story of one ship taken. He'd heard of a few brought back, taken, no doubt, from exploration ships. Now, was it to be war?

The debate went long and sometimes even loud as different courtiers took different sides. Some were for caution. "Wars cost blood and treasure."

Some, including the Imperial guard, were for war and glory.

Others cautiously voiced the fear that a lord who led a successful war might rise up and make war against his own neighboring satraps.

No one, of course, suggested that anyone would make war against the throne.

At least that was what they said. Did they, like the maiden, protest too much? Joseph must try to get his hands on more history. He and David were learning to read.

When the end came, it was sudden. In a rustling of cloth and the stomping of one foot, all fell silent.

"We would know more of these new things," came in a soft voice. "Kon'sum'We'sum'Quin Chap'sum'We, you will play with this new pet of yours and tell me if it can learn any tricks that might amuse our court. All of this kind who have fallen into our nets will be brought to you for your amusement, and maybe mine."

The Emperor here paused, then turned to his satrap lord. "My Servant, you may call out your ships and stuff them with crews to go forth for war. If you find glory, you may bring the tales of it back to me. If you fail us, know that you may make your apologies to us and your ancestors in person . . . and slowly."

The Lord of the Golden Satrap stood in place while the Emperor left in a flurry of cloth and curtains.

When the Emperor was gone, the lord snapped something at Roth's elders, then stomped out. They stayed on their knees for a long time as the army of courtiers whispered away on soft-soled shoes.

Only when the audience hall was silent did Roth whisper to Joseph, "If you can find the strength in your two legs to move, we can now leave."

With an effort, Joseph hauled himself to his feet. He made a profound bow to Roth, and his clan, then he waited while all of them left before following last, as should the least.

Joseph had heard many tales of war. He had never expected to be present when one was declared. "God help us," he prayed half aloud.

"Your God will need to help every human being alive or ever to be born," Roth added over his shoulder.

ABOUT THE AUTHOR

Mike Shepherd is the National best-selling author of the Kris Longknife saga. Mike Moscoe is the award nominated short story writer who has also written several novels, most of which were, until recently, out of print. Though the two have never been seen in the same room at the same time, they are reported to be good friends.

Mike Shepherd grew up Navy. It taught him early about change and the chain of command. He's worked as a bartender and cab driver, personnel advisor and labor negotiator. Now retired from building databases about the endangered critters of the Northwest, he's looking forward to some fun reading and writing.

Mike lives in Vancouver, Washington, with his wife Ellen, and not too far from his daughter and grandkids. He enjoys reading, writing, dreaming, watching grand-children for story ideas and upgrading his computer – all are never ending.

For more information:
www.mikeshepherd.org
mikeshepherd@krislongknife.com

2018 RELEASES

In 2016, I amicably ended my twenty-year publishing relationship with Ace, part of Penguin Random House.

In 2017, I began publishing through my own independent press, KL & MM Books. We produced six e-books and a short story collection. We also brought the books out in paperback and audio.

In 2018, I intend to keep the novels coming.

We will begin the year with **Kris Longknife's Successor**. Grand Admiral Santiago still has problems. Granny Rita is on the rampage again, and the cats have gone on strike, refusing to send workers to support the human effort on Alwa. Solving that problem will be tough. The last thing Sandy needs is trouble with the murderess alien space raiders. So, of course, that is what she gets.

May 1 will see **Kris Longknife: Commanding**. Kris has won her first battle, but the way the Iteeche celebrate victory can be hard on the stomach. The rebellion won't quit and now Kris needs to raise a fleet, not only to defend the Iteeche Imperial Capitol, but also take the war to the rebels.

In the second half of 2018, you can look forward to the next Vicky Peterwald novel on July 1, another Iteeche war novel on September 1, and **Kris Longknife Implacable** on November 1.

Stay in touch to follow developments by friending Kris Longknife and follow Mike Shepherd on Facebook or check in at my website www.krislongknife.com

2017 RELEASES

In 2016, I amicably ended my twenty-year publishing relationship with Ace, part of Penguin Random House.

In 2017, I began publishing through my own independent press, KL & MM Books.

I am delighted to say that you fans have responded wonderfully. We have sold over 20,000 copies of the five e-novels. In 2018, I intend to keep the novels coming,

We started the year with **Kris Longknife's Replacement** that tells the story of Grand Admiral Sandy Santiago as she does her best as a mere mortal to fill the shoes left behind on Alwa Station by Kris Longknife. Sandy has problems galore: birds, cats, and vicious alien raiders. Oh, and she's got Rita Nuu-Longknife as well!

February had a novelette. **Kris Longknife: Among the Kicking Birds** was part of Kris Longknife: Unrelenting. However, it went long and these four chapters were cut to one short paragraph. I hope you enjoy the full story.

Rita Longknife: Enemy Unknown was available in March and is the first book of the long-awaited Iteeche War series. Rita has had enough of Ray Longknife gallivanting around the universe. No sooner is little Al born, than ships start disappearing. Is it pirates or something more sinister? Rita gets herself command of a heavy cruiser, some nannies, and heads out to see what there is to see.

April had another short offering, **Kris Longknife's Bad Day**. You just knew when Kris asked for a desk job that she'd have days like you have at the office. Well, here's one that will bring you up to date on the technical developments in the Royal US Navy, as well as silly bureaucratic goings on. In the first draft of **Emissary**, these were the opening chapters, but I found a better opening and this got cut. Enjoy!

Kris Longknife: Emissary began an entirely new story arc for Kris and was available May 1. Here is the story of what it takes to get Kris out from behind a desk. And for those of you betting in the pool, you'll get your answer. More I cannot say.

June brought you Abby Nightingale's view of things around Alwa in **Kris Longknife's Maid Goes on Strike.** You knew sooner or later this was going to happen.

July had another book set in Alwa. As **Kris Longknife's Relief,** Sandy Santiago, continues to battle aliens of various persuasions and not a few humans.

Rita Longknife: Enemy in Sight was released in September and sought to resolve the unknowns left by Enemy Unknown as humanity slipped backwards into a war it does not want and may not be able to win.

Kris Longknife's Maid Goes on Strike and Other Short Stories, is a collection of four short stories: Maid Goes on Strike, Ruthie Longknife's First Christmas, Among the Kicking Birds, and Bad Day. These were available in October all under one ebook cover for a great price.

Kris Longknife: Admiral was available in November. In this adventure, Kris is up to her ears in warships, enemies, and friendlies who may be not as friendly as she'd like, as battlecruisers square off against battlecruisers. A fight where both sides are equal is a bloody fight that often no one wins.

Work is already going on for a January 18 release of Kris Longknife's Successor. March will have the next book in the Iteeche War, and May will continue Kris's adventures in the Iteeche Empire with Kris Longknife: Warrior.

Stay in touch to follow developments by following Kris Longknife on Facebook or checking in at my website www.mikeshepherd.org.

I hope to soon have a mailing list you can sign up for.